CANDIDE

CANDIDE
Or Optimism

Voltaire

WORDSWORTH CLASSICS

The paper in this book is produced from pure wood
pulp, without the use of chlorine or any other substance
harmful to the environment. The energy used in its
production consists almost entirely of hydroelectricity
and heat generated from waste materials, thereby
conserving fossil fuels and contributing little to the
greenhouse effect.

This edition published 1993 by
Wordsworth Editions Limited
8B East Street, Ware, Hertfordshire SG12 9HJ

ISBN 1 85326 063 0

Printed and bound in Denmark by Nørhaven

INTRODUCTION

Candide is Voltaire's greatest and most popular philosophical novel. It is a perceptive satire on the all-embracing optimism ('All is for the best in this best of all possible worlds') propounded by the German philosopher and mathematician Leibniz (1646-1716), It was published simultaneously in Amsterdam, Brussels, Geneva, London and Paris on 22 February 1759 and became a bestseller overnight. It is generally regarded as one of the great works of the Enlightenment – the liberal rationalist movement which swept across Europe in the 18h Century as a counterpoint to civil and ecclesiastical privilege– and a classic work in the literary history of the world.

   The publication of *Candide* was a masterful *coup* with four main aims: maximising publicity and royalties, frustrating pirate editions and flooding the market before the book could be suppressed. The plan succeeded brilliantly and *Candide* was not placed in the Vatican's 'Index of forbidden books' until 24 May 1762. Dr Pangloss, tutor to the hero, Candide, is used by Voltaire to personify the resolute optimist in *Candide*. Pangloss sticks to his beliefs through the direst events and evidence to contradict his faith. Misadventures begin when the young Candide is expelled from the Westphalian castle of Baron Thunder-ten-tronckt for making love to the Baron's daughter, Cunégonde. Following this, Candide, Cunégonde and Pangloss embark on a series of the most disastrous adventures which encompass Candide's conscription into the Bulgarian army, his fierce beating almost to death, being present for the terrible Lisbon earthquake on 1 November (All Saints Day) 1755, condemnation and pursuit by the Inquisition, his flight to El Dorado which he leaves loaded with riches only to have them swindled from him in France; and further travels to England, Venice and Turkey. Candide is finally reunited with Cunégonde and Pangloss and all three settle down on a small farm where Candide tells them 'we must cultivate our garden'. The manuscript version of *Candide* is now preserved in the Bibliothèque de l'Arsenal in Paris. Although also used by Boccaccio, Cervantes, Rabelais and Swift, the medium of the *conte philosophique* (philosophical tale) was one that Voltaire made his own.

Voltaire delights and dazzles the reader with his story-telling, while educating, challenging and instructing. His aim was to turn the 'brutish beasts' of received beliefs into the rational, questioning humanity which was the goal of the Enlightenment, and which has come to characterize our own age. His success can be measured by the continuing popularity of *Candide* to the present day.

Voltaire is the pseudonym of François-Marie Arouet the eminent French genius of the Enlightenment. He was noted as a correspondent, critic, dramatist, historian, moralist, novelist, poet, polemicist and satirist. Voltaire was relentless in his attacks on intolerance, evil, superstition and unjustified privileges – particularly those supported by the Church. Unusually, he combined literary and satirical skills with the abilities of a master story-teller. Born in Paris on 21 November 1694, Voltaire was the second son of a successful lawyer. His mother died when he was six years old and he was educated at the Jesuit college of Louis-le-Grand, a very highly regarded school. He became a law student but passed his time in smart, liberal society. In 1713 he was posted to the French embassy in Holland, but was summarily called home to prevent his eloping with a Protestant girl, Olympe Dunoyer. In 1716 he was suspected of writing a satire against the Regent, Phillipe d'Orléans, and internally exiled to Sully-sur-Loire. On 16/17 May the following year he was arrested and imprisoned in the Bastille without trial following another political satire. He was released in April 1718 and banished for six months to Châtenay, about six miles from Paris.

In June of that year he adopted the pseudonym – Voltaire – and in November staged his first major work, Oedipe, *to great acclaim. 1723 saw the publication of his epic poem on the subject of religious intolerance,* La Henriade *(about Henry of Navarre), which sealed his reputation as a literary colossus. He almost died of smallpox in the same year and was saved, as he observed, only by drinking huge quantities of lemonade. In 1726, after a fierce altercation with the aristocratic de Rohan family, he was again consigned to the Bastille prison in April and subsequently sent into exile abroad, in England in May.*

During Voltaire's exile in England (1726-1728) he discovered the work of the English scientist, Sir Isaac Newton, and met Bolingbroke, Pope and Swift. From 1729 and 1750 he lived in France and even enjoyed some favour at court with the support of Madame de Pompadour. He was elected as a Fellow of the Royal Society in London in 1743, and to membership of the Académie Française in 1746. His philosophical work, Zadig, was published in 1748, and he travelled to the court of Frederick of Prussia in June 1950. Micromégas was published in 1752. In 1759, the year of the publication of Candide Voltaire settled at the château de Ferney near Geneva where he was to live for the rest of his life. More publications appeared: Dictionnaire philosophique (1764), L'Ingénu (1767) and Le Taureau Blanc (1773-1774). In 1778 he returned to Paris for the production of his tragedy, Irène, and was fêted by the people of the French capital. It proved too great a strain and he died on 30 May. Fearing refusal of burial by the Church authorities, for so long the target of Voltaire's satire, his supporters smuggled his body out of Paris, to Scellières in Champagne, for burial. His remains were subsequently removed from Scellières in 1791, to lie in the Panthéon in Paris.

Further reading:
W H Barber: Voltaire – 'Candide' 1960
T Besterman: Voltaire 3/E 1976
W F Bottiglia: Voltaire's 'Candide' – Analysis of a classic 2/E 1966
H Mason: Voltaire – A Biography 1981

Contents

Part 1

I.	The Castle of Thunder-ten-Tronckh	1
II.	Running the Gauntlet	4
III.	Escape into Holland	6
IV.	Pangloss on the Pox	9
V.	The Death of the Anabaptist	12
VI.	An Auto-da-fé	15
VII.	Cunégonde Re-found	16
VIII.	Cunégonde's Story	19
IX.	Deaths of the Jew and the Inquisitor	22
X.	Embarkation for the New World	24
XI.	The Old Woman's Story – 1	26
XII.	The Old Woman's Story – 2	29
XIII.	The Governor of Buenos Aires	33
XIV.	Flight to Paraguay	35
XV.	The Jesuit Baron	39
XVI.	The Girls and the Monkeys	41
XVII.	El Dorado – 1	45
XVIII.	El Dorado – 2	48
XIX.	The Dutch Shipmaster	54
XX.	Martin the Manichaean	59
XXI.	The Nature of Mankind	62
XXII.	A Rich Stranger in Paris	64
XXIII.	'To Encourage the Others'	75
XXIV.	Paquette and Friar Giroflée	77
XXV.	Senator Pococurante	81

XXVI.	Supper with Six Kings	87
XXVII.	Voyage to Constantinople	91
XXVIII.	The Galley-slaves' Stories	95
XXIX.	Cunégonde Found Again	98
XXX.	Philosophy on the Propontis	99

PART II

I.	Candide Sets Out Again	109
II.	The Hospitable Persian	112
III.	A Favourite of the Sophi	115
IV.	Candide Loses a Leg	118
V.	Governor Candide	120
VI.	Candide's Seraglio	121
VII.	Zirza's Story	124
VIII.	The Abbé Again	127
IX.	Candide is Disgraced	130
X.	Pangloss and the Officer	133
XI.	The Newtonians *and* The Parricide	137
XIII.	Zenoida's Story	142
XIV.	The Wooing of Zenoida	145
XV.	Volhall Intervenes	148
XVI.	The Jealous Cunégonde	150
XVII.	Candide Meditates Suicide	153
XVIII.	The End of Pangloss	156
XIX.	The Last of Cunégonde	158
XX.	'Everything is Not Too Bad'	162

CANDIDE, or OPTIMISM

PART I

CHAPTER I

THE CASTLE OF THUNDER-TEN-TRONCKH

ONCE upon a time, in the province of Westphalia, at the castle of his lordship the Baron von Thunder-ten-Tronckh, there lived a boy of very sweet disposition. His mind could be read in his face. He was fairly intelligent, yet his general outlook was one of utter simplicity. Probably this was why he acquired the name of Candide.

The older servants of the household suspected that he was the son of his lordship's sister, the reputed father being a neighbouring landowner. The sister had refused to marry him, although he was an agreeable and worthy man, because his coat-of-arms had only seventy-one quarterings— the others having disappeared in the storms of time.

The Baron was one of the most powerful noblemen in Westphalia; as was evidenced by the fact that his castle had a great gate and windows, and its hall was hung with tapestry. The dogs that ran about his farms could at a pinch be mustered into a pack for hunting, at which his stablemen served as whippers-in. His grand chaplain was the village parson. Everyone called him 'My Lord', and laughed at his anecdotes.

Her ladyship the Baroness weighed about twenty-five stone. This contributed greatly to her prestige, which was enhanced by the dignity with which she did the honours of the house. The daughter, whose name was Cunégonde, was seventeen years old, fresh complexioned, plump, and attractive. The son of the house had the reputation of being 'a chip of the old block'.

The family had a household oracle, a tutor named Pangloss. Young Candide absorbed his teachings with the open-hearted simplicity of his age and nature. These teachings were metaphysico-theologo-cosmolonigological. Pangloss could prove to everybody's satisfaction that there is no effect without a cause: furthermore, that in this best of all possible worlds the Baron's castle was the finest of castles, and the Baroness the finest of all possible baronesses.

'It is demonstrable', Pangloss would say, 'that things cannot be other than they are. For, since everything is made for a purpose, everything must be for the best possible purpose. Noses, you observe, were made to support spectacles: consequently, we have spectacles. Legs, it is plain, were created to wear breeches, and are supplied with them. Stone was made to be quarried, and built into castles: that is why his lordship has such a fine castle—for the greatest baron in the province must of necessity also be the best housed. Pigs were made to be eaten: so we eat pork all the year round. It follows that those who say that *everything is good* are talking foolishly: what they should say is that *everything is for the best*.'[1]

Candide listened attentively to all this, and believed it. For his part, he thought Mistress Cunégonde extremely beautiful, though he never had the courage to tell her so. He concluded that, next to the happiness of being born a Baron von Thunder-ten-Tronckh, the second degree of happiness was to be Mistress Cunégonde; the third, to see

---

[1] In the French, '*tout est bien*' and '*tout est au mieux*'. This is the only passage in which Voltaire seems to indicate that there is any contradiction between the two phrases. Elsewhere Pangloss uses both as expressions of his doctrine, apparently almost interchangeably.

her every day; and the fourth, to be taught by Dr. Pangloss, the greatest philosopher in the province, and, therefore, in the whole world.

One day Cunégonde was walking near the castle, in the little copse which was known as 'the park', when through the bushes she saw Dr. Pangloss giving a lesson in applied physics to her mother's maid, a pretty and obliging little brunette. Having an inborn passion for natural science, Cunégonde, without betraying her presence, watched the Doctor's repeated demonstrations. She had no difficulty in understanding his 'sufficing reason'—a phrase that he often used—or the sequence of causes and effects. She returned home in a state of pensive agitation, filled with a desire for knowledge and reflecting that she herself might well become young Candide's 'sufficing reason'—and vice versa.

On her way back to the castle, she met Candide. She blushed, and greeted him in a faltering voice. Candide blushed too, and spoke without knowing what he said.

Next day, as they were leaving the table after dinner, Cunégonde and Candide found themselves behind a screen. Cunégonde dropped her handkerchief, and Candide picked it up. She artlessly seized his hand, and the youth artlessly kissed hers—with remarkable warmth, intensity and grace. Their lips met, their eyes sparkled, their knees trembled, their hands strayed . . .

Baron von Thunder-ten-Tronckh, who happened to pass by the screen, observed this interplay of cause and effect. He drove Candide out of the castle, with vigorous kicks from behind. Cunégonde fainted, and on coming to was smacked by the Baroness. There was consternation in the finest and best of all possible castles.

CHAPTER II

RUNNING THE GAUNTLET

EXPELLED from his earthly paradise, Candide wandered blindly and in tears, casting his eyes towards Heaven, or back towards the finest of castles, where lay the loveliest of barons' daughters. He lay down to sleep in a furrow; it was snowing heavily.

Next day, numb with cold, he dragged himself to the nearest village, which was called Valdberghofftrarbkdikdorff. Penniless and faint with hunger and fatigue, he loitered gloomily at the door of an inn.

He was observed by two men dressed in blue. 'Comrade,' said one of these, 'yonder is a well-made young fellow—of the right height, too.' They came up to Candide, and politely invited him to dine with them. 'Gentlemen,' said Candide, 'I am much honoured, but I have not the money for my share.'

'My dear young gentleman,' said one of the blue-coats, 'persons of your build and quality never pay for anything. Let me see, now, I reckon you would be five feet five inches high?'

'Yes, sirs, that is exactly my height', Candide bowed.

'Well, then, young gentleman, pray sit down with us. We will not only pay your reckoning, but will never suffer a man like you to want money. Men were born to assist one another.'

'You are perfectly right', said Candide. 'That is what Dr. Pangloss always says. I now see clearly that everything is for the best.'

His companions pressed several crowns upon him. He accepted, offering in exchange an I.O.U., which they declined to take. 'You are, I'll be bound, a man of loyalty and devotion?' said one of them.

'Yes, indeed, Mistress Cunégonde has all my ——'

'No, no, what we mean is, are you not loyally devoted to the King of Bulgaria?'

'Why, not at all, since I have never seen him.'

'But 'tis the most charming of kings! Come, we must drink to his health.' Candide drank to the toast.

'That's all that is required', he was then informed. 'You are now a mainstay, defender and hero of the Bulgarian people. Your fortune is made, you are on the high road to glory.'

Thereupon the two blue-coats put Candide in irons, and led him off to their regiment. He was taught to right turn, left turn, draw his rammer, return his rammer, present, fire, double quick march, and received thirty strokes with a cane. Next day he drilled a little less badly, and received only twenty strokes. On the third day he earned the admiration of his comrades by receiving only ten.

Candide was bewildered, and could not see how he was a hero. One fine spring day he decided to go for a walk—not to any place in particular—acting on the principle that human beings, like animals, have the right to use their legs as they wish. He had gone less than two leagues when he was overtaken by four other heroes, six feet tall, who tied him up and carried him to a prison cell.

At the court-martial, Candide was asked whether he preferred to run the gauntlet thirty-six times through the whole regiment, or to have his skull split by a dozen bullets. It was no use his saying that he didn't want either. He had to choose; so he exercised that divine gift known as 'Free Will' by choosing to run the gauntlet thirty-six times.

He performed two of these canters. Since the regiment numbered two thousand men, this meant four thousand

5

rammer blows, which laid his muscles and nerves bare from the neck to the rump.

As they were getting ready for the third lap, Candide gave up, and asked them, as a favour, to blow his brains out. The favour was granted. His eyes were bandaged, and he was told to kneel down.

At this moment the King of Bulgaria happened to pass by, and asked what the culprit had done. Being told, and being a monarch of genius, he realized that Candide was simply an unworldly young metaphysician, and pardoned him—for which act of clemency this king will no doubt be celebrated in all the newspapers and for all time.

A worthy surgeon healed Candide's wounds in three weeks, with salves originally prescribed by Dioscorides. By the time he had some of his skin back, and was able to walk, the King of Bulgaria was at war with the King of Abaria.

CHAPTER III

ESCAPE INTO HOLLAND

THE two armies were unrivalled for smartness of drill and turn-out, excellence of equipment and soundness of tactical disposition. Their trumpets, fifes, hautboys, drums and cannon made a music never heard in hell itself.

To start with, the artillery laid low about six thousand men on either side. After that, musket fire rid this best of all possible worlds of some nine to ten thousand of the scum of its surface. Finally, the bayonet was 'sufficing reason' for the deaths of some thousands more. The total number of deaths may have been about thirty thousand.

Candide shuddered, as a philosopher well might, and did his best to hide himself during the heroic butchery. At length—whilst, on the orders of the two kings, the *Te Deum* was being sung in both camps—he decided to go and continue his meditations on the nature of cause and effect in some other part of the world.

Passing over heaps of dead and dying, he came to a neighbouring village. It was in ashes, having been an Abarian village and therefore burnt, in accordance with the laws of war, by the Bulgarians. Old men mangled by bayonets watched their wives dying with gashes in their throats, clasping their children to their blood-stained breasts. Amongst the dying were girls who had been used to satisfy a number of heroes' natural needs, and had afterwards been disembowelled. Other women, half burnt alive, begged to be put out of their pain. The ground was covered with brains, arms and legs.

As fast as he could, Candide made off to another village. This one was Bulgarian, and the Abarian heroes had treated it in the same way.

Treading upon quivering limbs and rubble, Candide at length emerged from the theatre of war. His thoughts were still full of Mistress Cunégonde.

He had a small quantity of food in his haversack; but this had given out by the time he reached Holland. He had heard, however, that all the people of this country were rich, and expected to be as well treated there as he had been in the Baron's castle, up to the moment when Cunégonde's beauty had caused his expulsion.

He begged from several substantial-looking citizens, who told him that if he continued in this occupation he would be sent to a house of correction, to teach him how to live properly. At length he spoke to a man who, as it happened, had just been addressing a large gathering for over an hour on the subject of charity. The orator eyed him askance, and inquired: 'What brought you hither? Are you for the good cause?'

'Indeed, sir,' Candide answered shyly, 'I conceive that there can be no effect without a cause. Everything is bound upon a chain of necessity, and is arranged for the best. It was necessary that I should be driven from the presence of Mistress Cunégonde, and should run the gauntlet. Now it is necessary for me to beg my bread, until I can earn it. All this could not have been otherwise.'

'Hark ye, friend, do you hold the Pope to be anti-Christ?'

'I have never heard anyone say so. But whether he be or no, I am hungry.'

'Thou dost not deserve to eat. Hence, scoundrel! Away, wretch! Come not near me, for thy life!'

The orator's wife had been looking out of a window overhead. Seeing a man who doubted whether the Pope was anti-Christ, she emptied a chamberpot upon his head—an example of the excesses to which women are driven by religious zeal.

A man who had never been baptized, a kindly Anabaptist named James, witnessed this cruel and ignominious treatment of a fellow-man—a poor creature with two legs and a soul—and took Candide to his house, cleaned him up and gave him food and beer. Afterwards he gave him two florins, and even offered to teach him the trade of weaving Persian textiles—which, as it happens, are also manufactured in Holland.

Candide fell at James's feet, and exclaimed: 'My master Pangloss was in the right. Everything in this world is for the best. 'Tis plainly so, for I am much more affected by your generosity than I was by the harshness of the gentleman in the black cloak and his wife.'

CHAPTER IV

PANGLOSS ON THE POX

NEXT day, whilst out for a walk, Candide met a beggar covered with sores. The man's eyes were sunk in his head, the end of his nose eaten away, his mouth awry, his teeth black. He spoke in a husky whisper, coughed violently, and seemed to spit out a tooth at every spasm.

Candide felt even more pity than revulsion. He gave the horrible mendicant the two florins he had received from the Anabaptist; and then recoiled in dismay, as the apparition, gazing at him, burst into tears and fell on his neck.

'Alas,' said the poor creature, 'don't you know your poor Pangloss?'

'What, can it be you, my dear master—and in so fearful a plight? What disaster has befallen you? Why have you left the finest of castles? What is become of Mistress Cunégonde, that pearl amongst young ladies, that masterpiece of nature?'

'I am utterly spent', said Pangloss. Candide led him to the Anabaptist's stable, where he brought him something to eat. When Pangloss was feeling better, Candide resumed his questions: 'And now, pray, what of Cunégonde?'

'She is dead.'

Candide fainted. His friend rubbed his forehead with some stale vinegar which happened to be in the stable, and he reopened his eyes. 'Cunégonde dead! Ah, where is the best of worlds now? But of what illness did she die? Was it for grief upon seeing her father kick me out of the castle?'

'Bulgarian soldiers ravished her, and afterwards ripped open her belly. Her father sought to defend her, and they broke his skull. The Baroness was cut in pieces. My poor pupil was treated in exactly the same way as his sister. As for the castle, not one stone stands upon another. Not a barn remains, not a sheep, not a duck, not a tree.

'But we have had our revenge; for the Abarians have done the same in a neighbouring barony, which belonged to a Bulgarian lord.'

Candide fainted again. When he once more came to his senses, he inquired what causes and effects, what 'sufficing reason' had reduced Pangloss to his present piteous condition.

'Alas,' said Pangloss, 'it was love; love, the comfort of the human race, preserver of the universe, the soul of all feeling creatures; the tender passion of love.'

'Ah me,' said Candide, 'I too have known this love, sovereign of hearts, soul of our souls. All it brought me was one kiss, and a score of kicks on the backside. But how could so fair a cause produce in you so foul an effect?'

'Well, my dear Candide, you will remember Paquette, that pretty wench who waited on our august Baroness. In her arms I tasted those pleasures of paradise that produced the hellish torments with which you see me devoured. She suffered from an infection, and is perhaps now dead of it. She had it as a gift of a learned Franciscan friar, who derived it from the very fountain-head, since he had it of an old countess, who had it of a captain of horse, who had it of a marchioness, who had it of a page, who had it of a Jesuit, who, while yet a novice, had it in a direct line from one of the fellow-adventurers of Christopher Columbus.

'For my part, I shall give it to nobody, for I am dying.'

'Ah, Pangloss, what a sorry genealogy is that which you have described! Surely the devil was the root of it.'

'Not at all', replied the great man. 'It was a thing unavoidable, a necessary ingredient in the best of worlds; for if Columbus had not caught in an American isle this disease which poisons the spring of generation, and often even stops it, and is thus in itself evidently contrary to the great aim of nature, we should have neither chocolate nor cochineal.

'It is also to be observed that hitherto this malady is, like religious controversy, peculiar to our continent. The Turks, Indians, Persians, Chinese, Siamese and Japanese are not yet acquainted with it. There is, however, no doubt a sufficing reason why they, in their turn, should make its acquaintance within a few centuries.

'In the meantime, it is making amazing progress amongst us, and especially amongst those great and glorious armies that determine the fate of nations. One may safely affirm that, when two armies of 30,000 men each meet in battle, about 20,000 on either side have the pox.'

'That is all very interesting,' said Candide; 'but we must have you cured.'

'But how? I have not a penny, my friend, and nowhere on the surface of the globe can a man be bled or clystered without paying, or being paid for by another.'

Candide thereupon threw himself upon the mercy of the charitable Anabaptist James, and painted to him so striking a picture of his friend's condition that the good man at once took Dr. Pangloss into his house and paid for treatment for him. The result was that Pangloss lost only one eye and one ear. Since he wrote a good hand and was an excellent arithmetician, James made him his bookkeeper.

Two months later, James had to go on business to Lisbon, and took the two philosophers with him.

On the voyage, Pangloss explained to James the perfection of the scheme of things. James disagreed: 'Men must have deviated somewhat from their original innocence', he said. 'They were not born wolves, but they are become wolves. God did not give them twenty-four pounders nor bayonets, but they have made these things for their own destruction. I might also speak of bankruptcies, and the law which seizes upon the property of bankrupts solely in order to keep it from the creditors.'

'All that had to be', replied the one-eyed doctor. 'Private ills make up the general good. It therefore follows that, the more numerous the private ills, the greater the general good.'

As he spoke, the sky was darkening and a high wind was rising. The ship, which was now within sight of Lisbon harbour, was struck by a terrible storm.

CHAPTER V

THE DEATH OF THE ANABAPTIST

HALF of the passengers were so weak—torn by the abominable pangs that the rolling of a vessel shoots through the body's nerves and humours, which seem to clash together— that they could pay no heed to the danger. The other half screamed or prayed. The sails were in shreds, the mast broken, the ship gashed open. All efforts were useless, since no orders could be heard or given.

The Anabaptist, who was on deck trying to help, was knocked down by a frantic sailor, who himself was carried overboard, head first, by the force of his blow. His breeches caught on a broken mast, from which he dangled until James helped him back on board. James, in turn, was precipitated overboard by his effort, and fell into the sea in full view of the sailor, who calmly left him to drown.

Candide came on deck at this moment, and, seeing his benefactor going under for the third time, wanted to jump in after him; but he was restrained by Dr. Pangloss, who cogently argued that Lisbon roads had been specially contrived so that the Anabaptist might drown in them.

Whilst Pangloss was proving this point *a priori*, the ship broke up. Everyone was drowned except Pangloss, Candide and the brutal sailor. The latter swam to the shore, to which Pangloss and Candide were carried on a plank.

When they had recovered a little, they walked towards Lisbon. They still had some money, and hoped, having escaped from the storm, also to save themselves from starvation. Grieving for the death of their benefactor, they arrived at the outskirts of the city. At this moment the earth shook,[1] the sea rose up foaming in the harbour and dashed to pieces the ships lying at anchor. The streets and squares were filled with whirling masses of flame and cinders. The houses collapsed, the roofs crashing down on the shattered foundations. Thirty thousand inhabitants were crushed beneath the ruins.

The sailor whistled, and let out an oath. 'There's something to be got here', he remarked.

'What can be the sufficing reason for this phenomenon?' Pangloss wondered.

''Tis the day of judgment!' Candide exclaimed.

Risking death, the sailor dashed into the ruins in search of plunder. He found what he sought, got drunk, slept it off and then purchased the favours of the first obliging young woman he met—all this in the midst of ruined buildings and dead and dying people. Pangloss plucked his sleeve. 'Friend,' he said, 'this is not right. You trespass against the universal reason, and abuse your time.'

'Death and ounds!' the man replied. 'I am a sailor, and born in Batavia. In four voyages to Japan I have four times

[1] There was an earthquake, in which nearly 20,000 people were killed, at Lisbon on 1 November 1755.

trampled on the crucifix.[1] To the devil with you and your "universal reason"!'

Candide had been injured by flying stones, and was lying in the street covered with rubble. 'Alas!' he said to Pangloss, 'get me a little wine and oil, for I am dying.'

'This trembling of the earth's crust is no new thing', said Pangloss. 'The city of Lima, in America, experienced the same last year. Similar causes, similar effects. No doubt a subterranean train of sulphur stretches from Lima to Lisbon.'

''Tis very probable—but, for God's sake, a little oil and wine!'

'Probable! I maintain that the thing is proven.'

Candide fainted, and Pangloss brought him some water from a fountain near by.

Next day they found some food amongst the ruins, and, feeling rather stronger, joined in the work of giving aid to the survivors. Some of the citizens whom they had helped invited them to dinner. It was as good a meal as could be managed in the circumstances. The diners sat weeping over their plates, whilst Pangloss consoled them by explaining that things could not be otherwise. 'All this is for the best,' he said; 'since, if there is a volcanic eruption at Lisbon, then it could not have occurred in any other spot. It is impossible that things should be elsewhere than where they are; for everything is good.'

A little man dressed in black, who happened to be an agent of the Inquisition, was sitting next to Pangloss. 'It appears, sir,' he said suavely, 'that you do not believe in original sin; for, if everything is for the best, there can have been no fall or punishment of mankind.'

'I humbly beg your Excellency's pardon. The fall of man,

[1] In the seventeenth century, if a European shipmaster wished to enter a Japanese port, he and his crew were obliged to trample on a crucifix and declare that they were not Christians.

14

and the curse upon him, entered as a necessary part into the best of all possible worlds.'

'Then, sir, you do not believe in Free Will?'

'Your Excellency will excuse me. Free Will can subsist together with absolute necessity; for it was necessary that we should be free; for, indeed, the Determination of Will . . .'

The agent nodded to his henchman, who was pouring him out a glass of port.

CHAPTER VI

AN AUTO-DA-FÉ

AFTER the earthquake, which destroyed three-quarters of Lisbon, the country's leading thinkers decided that the best way of avoiding total destruction of the city was to give the people an *auto-da-fé*. The University of Coimbra was of the opinion that an infallible receipt for the prevention of earthquakes is the sight of some individuals being burnt over a slow fire.[1]

Amongst those arrested for the purpose was a Biscayan convicted of marrying his godmother, and two Portuguese who, whilst eating a chicken, had put the bacon that went with it on the edges of their plates. After dinner Dr. Pangloss and his disciple Candide were put in handcuffs: the former for what he had said, and the latter for having listened with an air of approval. They were led off to separate apartments—very cool ones, where they were in no danger of sunstroke.

A week later they were dressed in the Benedictine cassocks that are customary on such occasions, and paper mitres

---

[1] An auto-da-fé was held in Lisbon on 20 June 1756.

were put on their heads. Candide's cassock and mitre were painted with flames pointing downwards, and with devils that had no tails or claws; Pangloss's devils, on the other hand, had both these things, and his flames stood upright. They were led in a procession, and heard a very eloquent sermon, followed by an anthem sung in the *faux-bourdon* style of harmony. Candide was rhythmically flogged, in time to the singing. The Biscayan and the two men who did not like bacon were burnt. Pangloss was hanged—an unusual procedure at such ceremonies.

The same day there was another terrible earthquake.

Horrified, dumbfounded, bewildered, bleeding and gasping, Candide asked himself: 'If this is the best of all possible worlds, what can the others be like?' His own flogging he could bear with equanimity—he had suffered the same with the Bulgarians. But the hanging, for no comprehensible reason, of his beloved Pangloss, that greatest of philosophers; the drowning, in the very harbour, of the Anabaptist James, that best of men; and the evisceration of Mistress Cunégonde, that pearl amongst maidens: these were events whose necessity he could not understand.

As he was tottering feebly away from the place where he had been preached at, flogged, absolved and given benediction, an old woman came up to him and said: 'Be of good cheer, child, and follow me'.

CHAPTER VII

CUNÉGONDE RE-FOUND

CANDIDE was not at all of good cheer, but he followed the old woman. She led him to a hovel, where she gave him a pot of ointment, food and drink, and showed him to a clean little bed, beside which hung a suit of clothes. 'Eat, drink and sleep,' she said, 'and may Our Lady of Atocha, his lordship St. Anthony of Padua and his lordship St. James of Compostella watch over you. I shall be back tomorrow.'

Candide, who was still dazed by all that he had seen and suffered, and still more so by the old woman's kindness, sought to kiss her hand. 'It is not *my* hand you should kiss', she said. 'I shall be back tomorrow. Anoint your back, eat and sleep.'

Despite all his sorrows, Candide ate and slept. Next morning the old woman brought him breakfast, examined his back and rubbed it herself with another ointment. Later she brought him dinner and supper. The day after, she again brought him dinner. Candide kept on questioning her: who was she, what was the reason for all her kindness, how could he show his gratitude? But she did not answer.

On the evening of the second day, the old woman again came to Candide's room, but this time brought no supper. 'Come with me,' she said, 'and do not speak a word.' Taking him by the arm, she led him about a quarter of a mile into the country, to a lonely house surrounded by gardens and canals.

A small door was opened to her knock, and she led Candide by some back stairs to a small, gilt room, where she left him sitting on a brocaded sofa. Candide felt that his whole past life had been a nightmare, and that the present was also a dream, but a pleasant one.

In a short time the old woman came back, supporting a trembling young lady of majestic build, richly bejewelled and wearing a veil.

'Take off her veil', the old woman said, and Candide shyly did so. To his amazement, it was—yes, indeed, it was!—Mistress Cunégonde! He fell speechless at her feet, whilst she fell backwards upon the sofa. The old woman sprinkled them copiously with spirits, and they recovered enough composure to speak. At first they could utter only broken phrases, interrupting each other's questions and answers, gasping, weeping and exclaiming. The old woman advised them to make less noise, and left them alone.

'So it is really you,' said Candide, 'alive, and here in Portugal! So they did not ravish you, they did not rip your belly open?'

'Indeed they did', said Cunégonde. 'But these two accidents are not always mortal.'

'But were your father and mother killed?'

'Alas, it is but too true!' She wept.

'And your brother?'

'Yes, he too.'

'And how came you to Portugal? And how did you know that I was here? By what strange adventure did you contrive to have me brought to this house?'

'I will tell you the whole story. But first you must tell me what has befallen you, ever since the day when you gave me that innocent little kiss, and my father kicked you out of the castle.'

Candide made devoted haste to obey her. He was still in a state of bewilderment, and also somewhat distraught by the pain of his back, so that he spoke in a quavering whisper. He gave her a straightforward account of all that had happened to him since their separation. Cunégonde kept turning up her eyes in horror. She wept to hear of the death of the Anabaptist. Then she told her own story, whilst Candide avidly listened and gazed upon her.

CHAPTER VIII

CUNÉGONDE'S STORY

'I was fast asleep in bed when it pleased Heaven to send the Bulgarians to our castle. They slit the throats of my father and brother, and cut my mother in pieces. I fainted at the sight, and a strapping Bulgarian, six feet high, took the opportunity to ravish me.

'This brought me to my senses. I screamed, I struggled, I bit, I scratched, I would have torn the Bulgarian's eyes out. I did not know at this time that what was happening in my father's castle was all in accordance with the laws of war. The brute thrust a knife into my left side—I still bear the scar.'

'Alas, do let me see it!' said Candide ingenuously.

'You shall; but let me proceed.'

'Pray do.'

'A Bulgarian captain came into the room. He saw me lying there bleeding, and the soldier calmly continuing his operation. Angered by the man's failure to rise to his feet and salute, the captain killed him upon my body. He then had my wound dressed, and carried me, prisoner of war, to his quarters.

'I washed his few shirts and cooked his meals. I must confess that he thought me mighty handsome, and I shall not deny that he himself was very well made, with a white, smooth skin. For the rest, he was a dull man, with little knowledge of philosophy—not at all like a pupil of Dr. Pangloss.

'Three months later the captain had grown tired of me. Having lost all his money at play, he sold me to a Jew named Don Issachar, who traded to Holland and Portugal, and was passionately fond of women. This Jew took a great liking for my person, but could not prevail over it. I resisted him better than I had resisted the Bulgarian soldier. A chaste woman may be ravished once, but her virtue is all the stronger for it.

'To tame me to his desires, the Jew then brought me to this place. I had believed that nothing could equal the beauty of Thunder-ten-Tronckh, but my eyes have been opened.

'One day, while at Mass, I was observed by the Grand Inquisitor. He ogled me throughout the service, and afterwards sent me a message that he wished to speak with me on private business. I was led to his palace, where I told him my origin. He represented to me how much beneath my rank it was to belong to an Israelite, and sent an intermediary to Don Issachar with the proposal that he should yield me to his lordship.

'Don Issachar, who is a court banker and a man of standing, refused to do anything of the sort, and the Inquisitor threatened him with an *auto-da-fé*. The upshot was that my Jew came to a composition, whereby this house and myself should belong to the two of them jointly. The Jew was to be the owner on Tuesday, Thursday and the Jewish Sabbath, the Inquisitor on the other days of the week.

'This arrangement has been in force for six months, but not without disputes; for they often fail to agree as to whether the night from Saturday to Sunday comes under the old law or the new. For my part, I have hitherto withstood both of them—and that, I think, is the reason why they still love me.

'It came about that, in order to avert the scourge of the earthquakes, and also to intimidate Don Issachar, my Lord Inquisitor was pleased to hold an *auto-da-fé*. He did me the honour of inviting me to be present, and I had a very good seat. In the interval between Mass and the executions, the ladies were served with refreshments.

'I assure you that I was dreadfully shocked at the burning

of the two Jews, and of that poor Biscayan who had married his godmother. But what was my amazement and horror when I saw, in Benedictine cassock and mitre, a figure resembling Pangloss! I rubbed my eyes, gazed at him closely, and saw him hanged. I swooned away.

'Scarce had I recovered my senses, when I beheld you stripped naked. That was the height of my horror, consternation, grief and despair. I will confess to you that your skin is even whiter and more blooming than that of my Bulgarian captain. The sight enhanced the pangs of grief that were crushing and gnawing at me. I shrieked, I wanted to cry out: "Hold, barbarians!" But my voice failed me, and in any case it would have done no good.

'After your flogging, I said to myself: "To think that my dear Candide and wise old Pangloss should be here in Lisbon, the one to receive a hundred lashes and the other to be hanged, and all on the orders of my Lord Inquisitor—and he my suitor! 'Twas a cruel lie that Pangloss told me when he said that everything in this world is for the best!"

'Agitated and bewildered, now in a frenzy and now half dead with weakness, I kept thinking of the massacre of my father, mother and brother; of the insolence of that villainous Bulgarian soldier and the wound he dealt me; of my servitude and employment as a cook-wench; of my wretched Don Issachar and horrible Inquisitor; of that swelling *Miserere* that was sung while you were being flogged; and especially, again and again, of that kiss you gave me behind the screen, on the day I saw you for the last time.

'I praised God for bringing you back to me after so many trials, and ordered my old attendant to take care of you and to bring you hither as soon as she might. She has carried out my orders well, and I have the inexpressible delight of seeing you again.

'But you must be ravening with hunger; and I, too, have a great appetite. Let us first have supper.'

They sat down at table, and after supper returned to the magnificent sofa already mentioned. They were still there when Don Issachar entered. It was the Sabbath day, and he had come to exercise his rights and expatiate upon his tender passion.

CHAPTER IX

DEATHS OF THE JEW AND THE INQUISITOR

ISSACHAR was the quickest-tempered Hebrew since the Babylonian captivity. 'How now, thou Galilean bitch!' he said. 'Is not the Inquisitor enough for thee, that I must also share thee with this rascal? He drew a long poniard, which he always carried, and rushed at Candide, thinking him to be unarmed. But the stalwart young Westphalian had received, along with the suit of clothes that the old woman gave him, an excellent sword. Despite his naturally gentle and peaceable nature, he drew, and laid the Israelite stone dead at the fair Cunégonde's feet.

'Holy Virgin!' she cried. 'What will become of us? A man killed in my apartment! If the peace-officers come, we are undone!'

'Had Pangloss not been hanged,' Candide replied, 'that great philosopher would have given us good advice in this emergency. Since we have not him, let us consult the old woman.'

She was a shrewd old lady, and very willing to give advice. As she was doing so, the door again opened. It was an hour after midnight, and therefore the beginning of Sunday, a day which belonged to my Lord Inquisitor. He was now confronted with Candide, that recently flogged felon, standing with drawn sword; a corpse on the ground; Cunégonde cowering with fright; and the old woman giving her advice.

The train of thought that now passed clearly and rapidly through Candide's mind ran as follows: 'If this holy man calls for assistance, he will certainly have me burnt, and perhaps Cunégonde too. He has had me cruelly whipped. He is my rival. I have set out on a career of slaughter. There is no time to hesitate.' Before the Inquisitor could recover from his surprise, Candide ran him through the body, and laid him beside the Jew.

'And now there's another of them!' wailed Cunégonde. 'This is unpardonable, we are excommunicated, our last hour is come! But how could you—you, who are of so mild a temper—bring yourself to kill a Jew and a prelate, all in two minutes?'

'Beautiful Mistress,' said Candide, 'when a man is in love, is jealous, and has been flogged by the Inquisition, he does the most surprising things.'

'There are three Andalusian horses in the stable,' said the old woman, 'with their saddles and bridles. Let Candide make them ready. Madam has some moidores and diamonds. Let us get quickly to horse—though, for my part, I have only one buttock to sit upon—and be off to Cadiz. The weather is as fine as could be, and 'tis a great pleasure to travel in the cool of the night.'

Candide at once saddled the three horses, and they covered thirty miles without stopping. Meanwhile the Holy Brotherhood entered Issachar's house, buried his lordship in a fine church, and threw Issachar on a dunghill.

By this time Candide, Cunégonde and the old woman were already at an inn in the little town of Aracena, in the Sierra Morena, where they were engaged in an earnest discussion.

CHAPTER X

EMBARKATION FOR THE NEW WORLD

CUNÉGONDE wept. 'Who can have taken them?' she said. 'What shall we live on? What are we to do?' Her moidores and diamonds had disappeared. 'Where can I find a Jew or an Inquisitor to give me some more?' she sobbed.

'I strongly suspect a certain reverend Franciscan friar', said the old woman. 'He lay last night in the same inn with us at Badajoz. God preserve me from making hasty judgments, but he came into our room twice, and left the inn long before us.'

'Ah me,' said Candide, 'Pangloss often used to demonstrate that the world's goods are common to all men, and that each has an equal right to them. But, even according to this principle, the friar should have left us enough to carry us to the end of our journey. Have you nothing left at all, dearest Cunégonde?'

'Not a stiver.'

'Then what is our course of action?'

'Sell one of the horses', said the old woman. 'I will ride on the crupper behind Mistress Cunégonde, though I have only one buttock to ride on, and we shall reach Cadiz.'

A Benedictine prior who was lodging at the inn bought the horse very cheap. They rode through Lucena, Chillas and Lebrija, and arrived at Cadiz.

Here a fleet was being equipped, and troops raised, to teach a lesson to the reverend Jesuit Fathers of Paraguay. The Jesuits were accused of having stirred up one of their Indian tribes, in the area of San Sacramento, to revolt against the Kings of Spain and Portugal.

Profiting from his service with the Bulgarians, Candide

went through the drill of that army in the presence of the Spanish general. He displayed so much smartness, speed, initiative, morale and efficiency that he was given command of a company. Thus, as a captain, he was able to take on board with him Cunégonde, the old woman, two valets and the Grand Inquisitor's horses.

During the voyage they spent much time discussing poor Pangloss's doctrines. 'We are going to another world,' said Candide, 'and doubtless it is in this new world that everything is good; for I must confess that events in the world we have known, both physical and spiritual, have been enough to make one tremble a little.'

'I love you with all my heart', said Cunégonde. 'But nonetheless I am still scared to the depths of my soul by all that I have seen and undergone.'

'All will be well. Why, the seas of this new world are already better than the seas of Europe. They are smoother, and the winds are steadier. For certain, it is this new world that will prove to be the best of all possible ones.'

'God grant it. But I have been so horribly unhappy in the world I have known, that my heart is almost shut against hope.'

'You moan and complain,' said the old woman, 'but you have not suffered half what I have done.'

Cunégonde could hardly help laughing at this seemingly ridiculous assertion. 'My good dame,' she said, 'unless you have been ravished by two Bulgarians—stabbed in the stomach twice over—seen two of your castles demolished, two mothers and two fathers having their throats cut, and two lovers flogged at an *auto-da-fé*—I do not see how you can claim to have endured twice as much misery as I have. Add to this, that I was born a baroness, with seventy-two quarterings, and have since been a cook-wench.'

'Mistress, I have never told you my origin. And if I were to show you my backside, you would not speak so hastily.'

Cunégonde and Candide were eager to know what the old woman meant. She told them her story as follows.

CHAPTER XI

THE OLD WOMAN'S STORY—1

'MY eyes were not always bloodshot and red-rimmed; my nose did not always touch my chin; nor was I always a servant.

'I am the daughter of Pope Urban X[1] and the Princess of Palestrina. Until the age of fourteen I was brought up in a castle to which none of the castles of your German princes would serve as stables. A single one of my robes was worth more than all the treasure in Westphalia.

'I grew in beauty, grace and talent, in the midst of pleasures, homage and fair expectations. Already I inspired men with love. Already my bosom was forming—and what a bosom! White, firm and shaped like that of the Venus of the Medicis. My eyebrows were black, my eyes flashed brighter than the stars—or so our poets told me. The women who dressed and undressed me fell into ecstasies when they beheld me before and behind; and all the men would willingly have changed places with them.

'I was betrothed to a ruling Prince of Massa Carrara. Such a prince! As handsome as myself, crammed full of sweetness and charm, brilliantly witty and aflame with love. I loved him as one loves for the first time—with idolatrous fervour.

[1] 'Observe the extreme discretion of the author. There has until now been no Pope named Urban X. The author is unwilling to attribute a bastard to any known Pope. What circumspection! What delicacy of conscience!'—Note by Voltaire.

'The nuptials were to be of unprecedented pomp and magnificence, with festivities, roundabouts and light operas. All Italy composed sonnets in my praise—all of them execrable. The moment of my supreme happiness was at hand, when an old marquesa, who had been my prince's mistress, invited him to take chocolate with her. He died less than two hours later, in frightful convulsions.

'But that was a mere trifle. My mother, who was in despair, although her affliction was less than mine, resolved to remove herself for a while from the scene of tragedy. She had a fine estate near Gaeta, for which we embarked on a galley gilt, in the fashion of my country, like the high altar of St. Peter's at Rome. In our passage we were boarded by a Sali corsair. Our men fought like soldiers of the Pope—that is, they flung themselves on their knees, laid down their arms and begged the corsair to give them absolution *in articulo mortis*.

'They were forthwith stripped as naked as apes; as also were my mother, our maids of honour and myself. It is amazing how expert these gentry are at undressing people. But what astonished me more was that they thrust their fingers into a region where we women as a rule allow only —— to enter. At first I thought this very strange—it is remarkable how travel broadens the mind—but I later learnt that the purpose was to discover if we had concealed any diamonds. The practice has been established from time immemorial among the highly efficient nations that scour the seas. I have been told that the religious Knights of Malta never neglect it when they capture Turks of either sex. It is a part of the law of nations, from which they never deviate.

'I need not tell you how hard it is for a young princess and her mother to be led off to slavery in Morocco. You can likewise imagine what we had to suffer on board the corsair. My mother was still very handsome, and our maids of honour, and even our common waiting women, had more charms than are to be found in all Africa. As to myself, I was enchanting; I was beauty and grace itself—and I was a maid. I did not remain one long; the flower that had been reserved for the Prince of Massa Carrara was snatched from me by the corsair captain, a hideous negro, who positively thought that he was doing me an honour.

'Indeed, both the Princess of Palestrina and myself must have had very strong constitutions to withstand all that we endured till our arrival at Morocco. But I shall not waste time on further relating such commonplace matters.

'At the time of our arrival, Morocco was being deluged with blood. Fifty sons of the Emperor Muley Ishmael were each at the head of a faction. Thus fifty different civil wars were in progress—blacks against blacks, mulattoes against blacks, and mulattoes against mulattoes. The whole empire was a field of continual slaughter.

'As soon as we landed, a party of blacks of a faction hostile to that of our captain, came to take away his booty. Next to his diamonds and gold, we were the most valuable things he had. A battle ensued, such as you never see in your European climates. The northern peoples have not the hot blood, nor the raging lust after women, of the African. It seems to be milk that runs in European veins, compared with the vitriol and flame that gush through the veins of the inhabitants of Mount Atlas and the neighbouring lands. They fought with the fury of the lions, tigers and serpents of their country, to know who should have us. A Moor seized my mother by the right arm, my captain's lieutenant seized her by the left arm, another Moor took her by the right leg and one of our corsairs by the left. Almost all our women were thus torn between four men.

'My captain kept me hidden behind him, and with drawn scimitar slew all who stood in his way. The end of it was that my mother and all our Italian women were torn to pieces by the monsters who contended for them. Captives and captors, soldiers and sailors, blacks, whites and mulattoes, and lastly my captain himself, were all slain, and I was left half dead upon a heap of carcases.

'Similar scenes were being enacted over a region more than three hundred leagues in length; yet there was never any failure to observe the five daily prayers enjoined by Mahomet.

'I disengaged myself with difficulty from the pile of bloody corpses, and dragged myself beneath a large orange tree on the bank of a near-by stream. Here I collapsed from fright, weariness, horror, despair and hunger, and my crushed senses yielded to an oblivion that was rather a swoon than a sleep.

'In this state of weakness and insensibility, between life and death, I felt myself pressed upon by something that moved up and down on my body. Opening my eyes I saw a white man, of good appearance, who was sighing and muttering: "*O che sciagura d'essere senza coglioni!*"

CHAPTER XII

THE OLD WOMAN'S STORY—2

'Astonished and delighted to hear the speech of my country, and not less surprised at the man's words, I told him that there were heavier misfortunes than what he complained of. I briefly described to him the horrors that I had passed through, and fell back into my swoon.

'The man carried me to a house, where he had me put to bed and given food. He waited on me, comforted and flattered me, vowing that he had never seen anything so beautiful as myself, and had never before so much regretted the loss of what no one could restore to him.

'"I was born at Naples," he said, "where they caponize two or three thousand children every year. Some die; others acquire voices more beautiful than women's; and others become Governors of states.[1] In my case, the operation was a great success, and I was one of the singers in the Princess of Palestrina's chapel."

'"How," cried I, "in my mother's chapel!"

'"What, is the Princess of Palestrina your mother?" he exclaimed, and burst into tears. "Then you are the little princess whom I had the care of until she was six years old. Already at that age she promised to be as beautiful as you."

'"Yes, 'tis I. My mother lies four hundred yards hence, torn in four pieces, beneath a heap of dead. . ."

'We exchanged accounts of our adventures. A certain Christian state had sent him as envoy to the King of Morocco, to conclude a treaty with that monarch whereby he was to be furnished with powder, guns and ships to help him to destroy the commerce of other Christians.[2]

'"My mission has been accomplished", said the eunuch. "I am going to take ship at Ceuta, and will escort you back to Italy. *Ma che sciagura d'essere senza coglioni!*"

'I thanked him, with tears of joy. Thereupon, instead of conducting me to Italy, he carried me to Algiers, where he sold me to the Dey.

'Soon afterwards the plague, which had made the tour of Africa, Asia and Europe, began raging in Algiers. You have seen earthquakes, mistress; but tell me, had you ever the plague?'

[1] Ferdinand VI appointed a Neapolitan eunuch named Farinelli to be a Governor in Spain.

[2] During the War of the Spanish Succession the King of Portugal sent such an envoy to Morocco.

'No', said Cunégonde.

'If you had, you would confess that an earthquake is a trifle to it—and it is very common in Africa.'

'I was one of those seized with it. Picture to yourself the plight of a Pope's daughter, fifteen years old, who within three months had suffered want and slavery, had been ravished almost daily, had seen her mother torn into four pieces, had passed through famine and war, and was now dying of the plague in Algiers!

'In the end, I did not die; but my eunuch, and the Dey, and almost the whole seraglio of Algiers, were swept off.

'When the plague had spent its first fury, a sale was made of the Dey's slaves. A merchant bought me, and carried me to Tunis. There he sold me to another merchant, by whom I was sold again at Tripoli. From Tripoli I was sold to Alexandria, thence to Smyrna, and thence to Constantinople, where I became the property of an aga of the Janissaries.

'This aga was ordered away to the defence of Azov, which was besieged by the Russians.[1] Being a great affecter of the fair sex, he took his whole seraglio with him into the field. We were lodged in a small fort upon the Maeotic Swamp, under guard of two black eunuchs and twenty soldiers.

'Our army made a great slaughter among the Russians, but they repaid us well in kind. Azov was reduced to blood and ashes; no quarter was given on grounds either of age or of sex.

'At length only our little fort was left. The enemy sought to reduce it by starvation. The twenty Janissaries, who had sworn never to surrender, were obliged to eat the two eunuchs, rather than break their oath. A few days later, they resolved to eat the women.

'We had with us a very devout imam, who in an eloquent

[1] Azov was besieged by the Russians in 1739.

sermon persuaded them not to kill us outright. "Only cut off one of the buttocks of each of these ladies," he said, "and you will find an excellent meal. If need be, you can in a few days have recourse to its fellow. Heaven will smile upon so charitable an action, and you will be relieved."

'His eloquence persuaded them, and we were subjected to this fearsome operation. The imam applied the same ointment as is used on newly circumcised children. We were all at death's door.

'Just when the Janissaries had finished the repast with which we had supplied them, the Russians attacked in flat-bottomed boats, and every single Janissary was killed.

'The Russians paid no heed to our plight. But they had with them a French surgeon—such people are found everywhere—a man of great skill, who took care of us and healed us. I shall always remember that no sooner were my wounds closed than he made advances to me. He also sought to cheer us by explaining that the like had happened in many sieges, and was in full conformity with the laws of war.

'As soon as my companions and I could walk, we were sent to Moscow. I fell to the lot of a boyar, who set me to work in his garden, and gave me twenty lashes a day. Two years later this nobleman, with some thirty others, was broken on the wheel as a result of a court feud. I took advantage of this event to escape.

'After making my way across Russia, I for a long time served as chambermaid at inns at Riga, Rostock, Wismar, Leipzig, Cassel, Utrecht, Leyden, the Hague and Rotterdam. I grew old in poverty and degradation, with only the half of a backside, and remembering always that I was a Pope's daughter. A hundred times I wished to kill myself, but my love of life persisted. This ridiculous weakness is perhaps one of the most fatal of our faults. For what could be more stupid than to go on carrying a burden that we always long to lay down? To loathe, and yet cling to, existence? In short, to cherish the serpent that devours us, until it has eaten our hearts?

'In the countries through which my destiny led me, and in the inns where I served, I saw a prodigious number of people who hated their existence. Yet only twelve of them voluntarily put an end to it: namely, three negroes, four Englishmen, four Genevans and a German professor named Robeck.

'My last place was with the Jew, Don Issachar, who set me to attend upon you, my fair lady. I have attached myself to your fortunes, and have been more concerned with your adventures than with my own. I should not have even spoken to you of my mishaps had you not provoked me a little, and were it not customary on shipboard to pass the time by telling stories.

'In short, mistress, I know much of the world. Divert yourself by inducing each passenger to tell you his story; and if there is a single one of them who has not many times cursed his life, and sworn that he was the most wretched of men, I give you leave to throw me head foremost into the sea.'

CHAPTER XIII

THE GOVERNOR OF BUENOS AIRES

AFTER hearing the old woman's story Cunégonde paid her the respect due to a person of her rank and merits. On her suggestion, she induced all the passengers, one after another, to relate their adventures; and she and Candide had to admit that the old woman was right.

''Tis a sad pity,' said Candide, 'that wise old Pangloss was hanged—and how such a thing could happen at an *auto-da-fé*, I don't know—since he might have discoursed to us admirably on the physical and moral evils that overspread the earth and sea; and I should have been bold enough to offer some few respectful objections.'

On reaching Buenos Aires, Cunégonde, Captain Candide and the old woman paid a visit to the Governor. He was called Don Fernando d'Ibarro y Figueora y Mascarenes y Lampourdos y Souza, and his behaviour befitted a man with so many names. In conversation with men, his air of noble disdain, uptilted nose, excruciatingly affected accent and stilted manner made everyone long to hit him. For women he had an insatiable passion.

Cunégonde seemed to the Governor the most beautiful thing he had ever seen. He inquired whether she was the Captain's wife. His manner alarmed Candide, who dared not say that she was his wife—since she was not; nor that she was his sister—since she was not that either. Although a useful lie of this sort would have had many historical precedents, Candide was too open-hearted for such deceit. 'Mistress Cunégonde', he said, 'intends to do me the honour to marry me—and we beg your Excellency to condescend to grace the ceremony with your presence.'

Don Fernando d'Ibarro y Figueora y Mascarenes y Lampourdos y Souza twirled his moustache, smiled sourly and ordered Captain Candide to go and inspect his company. Left alone with Cunégonde, he declared his passion, and swore that he would marry her next day—in church or otherwise, her beauty was such that it was all one to him.

Cunégonde asked for a quarter of an hour's reflection. She wanted to ask advice of the old woman.

'Mistress,' said the old woman, 'you have seventy-two quarterings, but not a penny. If you choose, you can be the wife of the greatest nobleman in South America—with a very fine moustache, too. Is it for you to pride yourself upon an unshakable fidelity? You have been ravished by the Bulgarians. A Jew and an Inquisitor have enjoyed your favours. Misfortunes carry their own privileges. If I were you, I should have no hesitation in marrying the Governor —and making the Captain's fortune.'

That same day a small ship entered the harbour of Buenos Aires, carrying an alcayde and a party of alguazils. The reason for their arrival was as follows:

As the old woman had guessed, the thief of Cunégonde's money and jewels at Badajoz had been a Franciscan friar. This man had tried to sell some of the stones to a jeweller, who had recognized them as the property of the Grand Inquisitor. Before being hanged, the friar confessed his theft, and had described the persons whom he had robbed and the road they were taking. The flight of Cunégonde and Candide was by this time known. They were pursued to Cadiz, and thence across the ocean. The pursuing ship had now arrived in Buenos Aires harbour; and already the report had spread that it had an alcayde aboard, and had come for the murderers of his lordship the Grand Inquisitor.

The clever old woman realized the situation at once. 'You cannot run away,' she said to Cunégonde, 'and you have nothing to fear. It was not you who killed his lordship. Besides, as the Governor is in love with you, he will not suffer you to be ill-treated. Stand your ground.'

Then she hurried to Candide. 'Flee,' she said, 'or you will be burnt alive within the hour.'

He had not a moment to lose. But how could he bring himself to part from Cunégonde, and where was he to go?

CHAPTER XIV

FLIGHT TO PARAGUAY

CANDIDE had brought with him from Cadiz a valet of a type that is common along the coasts of Spain and in the colonies. He was only one quarter Spanish, having been born in Tucuman of a mestizo father. He had been at various times a choirboy, a sacristan, a sailor, a monk, a shop-boy, a soldier and a lacquey. His name was Cacambo, and he had a great affection for Candide—which, indeed, the latter well deserved.

Cacambo quickly saddled the two Andalusian horses. 'Come, master,' he said, 'let us take the old woman's advice, and be off without more ado.'

'My dearest Cunégonde,' said Candide, weeping, 'must I leave you in the very moment the Governor was going to preside at our wedding? What will become of you, so far from home?'

'She must do as well as she can', said Cacambo. 'Women can always look after themselves. God provides for them. Let us be off.'

'But whither wilt thou carry me? Where can we go? What shall we do without Cunégonde?'

'By St. James of Compostella! You were on your way to fight the Jesuits; let us fight on their side. I know the roads, and can lead you to their kingdom. They will be delighted to have a captain who knows Bulgarian drill and tactics. You will make a vast fortune. When one cannot come to terms with one world, one can always do so with another. 'Tis a great delight to see and do new things.'

'Then you have been in Paraguay?'

'Ay, marry, have I! I was a scout in the College of the Assumption, and I know the domain of *los padres* as well as I know the streets of Cadiz. And what an admirable domain it is! The kingdom is already upwards of three hundred leagues in diameter, and divided into thirty provinces. *Los padres* own everything, the tribes nothing. 'Tis a masterpiece of rational and just rule! Why, I know of nothing so near to divine Almightiness as *los padres*: here they make war against the kings of Spain and Portugal, and over in Europe they receive these same kings in their confessionals. Here they kill Spaniards, and over there they speed them on their way to Heaven: 'tis exquisite!

'But let us make haste; you have rare good fortune in store for you. How pleased *los padres* will be to learn that they are getting a captain who knows Bulgarian drill and tactics!'

When they reached the first frontier barrier, Cacambo told the outpost that a captain wished to speak with his lordship the commandant. The main guard was turned out, and a Paraguayan officer ran to kneel before the commandant and report the news to him. Candide and Cacambo were immediately disarmed, and their horses were seized. They were led, between two files, towards the commandant, who wore a three-cornered hat and a tucked-up habit, had a sword by his side and carried a half-pike. He gave a sign, and the newcomers were surrounded by twenty-four soldiers. A sergeant told them that they must wait; the commandant could not speak with them, since the Reverend Father Provincial did not allow any Spaniard to speak except in his presence, or to remain in the country for more than three hours.

'Where is the Reverend Father Provincial?' Cacambo asked.

'He has said Mass, and is on parade. You will not be able to kiss his spurs for another three hours.'

'But the Captain and I are perishing with hunger; and the Captain is no Spaniard, but a German. Could we not eat while we wait for his Reverence?'

The sergeant immediately reported what he had been told to the commandant. 'God be praised!' said the latter. 'If he is a German, I may speak with him. Let him be brought to my arbour.'

Candide was conducted to a bower adorned with a

pretty colonnade of green and yellow marble, and with cages containing parrots, humming-birds, guinea-fowl, and birds of other rare kinds. An excellent breakfast was waiting in gold vessels. Whilst his Paraguayan troops ate maize from wooden trenchers in the blazing sun, the Reverend Father Commandant entered the arbour.

He was a very handsome young man, round-faced, fair and freshly coloured, with finely arched eyebrows, bright eyes, pink ears and red lips. He carried himself boldly, with a bearing that was neither Spanish nor Jesuit. On his orders Candide and Cacambo were given back their arms and horses. Cacambo had oats brought for the animals, and tethered them close to the arbour, where he kept his eye on them for fear of some trickery.

Candide kissed the hem of the Commandant's robe, and they sat down to table. 'So you are a German?' said the Jesuit, in that language.

'Yes, Reverend Father.' The two men suddenly looked at each other with amazement and emotion.

'From what part of Germany do you come?'

'From Westphalia. I was born in the castle of Thunder-ten-Tronckh.'

'Oh, heavens, can it be?'

'What a miracle!'

'Can it be you?'

'It is not possible!' They both reeled backwards, and then embraced, weeping.

'So you, Reverend Father, are the fair Cunégonde's brother! But I thought you were slain by the Bulgarians. But how come you, the Baron's son, to be a Jesuit in Paraguay? What a strange world! Ah, Pangloss, what joy this would have given you, if you had not been hanged!'

The negro and Paraguayan slaves, who were serving wine in crystal goblets, withdrew on the commandant's order.

With exclamations of praise to God and St. Ignatius, he clasped Candide in his arms. Their faces were wet with tears.

'You will be still more overcome', said Candide, 'when I tell you that Mistress Cunégonde, your sister, has not been disembowelled, as you supposed, but is in perfect health.'

'Where is she?'

'Not far from here, at the house of the Governor of Buenos Aires. I came here to fight you.'

Throughout a long conversation, they continued to marvel more and more, talking volubly and hanging on each other's words, with shining eyes. In German fashion, they lingered long at table, waiting for the Reverend Father Provincial. Meanwhile the commandant told his story:

CHAPTER XV

THE JESUIT BARON

'I SHALL never forget the dreadful day when I saw my father and mother slain, and my sister ravished. When the Bulgarians went, my sister was nowhere to be found. The bodies of my parents and myself, with those of the servant maids and of three little boys, all of whose throats had been cut, were thrown upon a cart, to be buried in a Jesuit chapel that lies two leagues from the castle.

'A Jesuit sprinkled us with holy water. It was dreadfully salt, and a few drops of it went into my eyes. The Father saw my eyelids stir, put his hand on my heart and felt it beating. I was cared for, and in three weeks was completely recovered.

'As you will remember, my dear Candide, I was a very handsome lad. I became still more so, and the Reverend Father Croust, Superior of the House, took a great fancy to me. He gave me the novice's habit, and in a short time I was sent to Rome. Our Genera was recruiting young German Jesuits. The rulers of Paraguay admit as few Spanish Jesuits as possible; they prefer those of other nations, as being more easily governed. The Reverend Father General considered me a fit person to come and labour in this vineyard. I set out with a Pole and a Tyrolese, and on arrival was given a subdeaconship and a lieutenancy. I am now a priest and a colonel.

'We shall give a warm reception to the King of Spain's troops, I can assure you. They will be beaten first, and excommunicated afterwards. Providence has sent you hither to assist us.

'But is it really true that my sister Cunégonde is with the Governor of Buenos Aires?' Candide solemnly assured him that it was so, and again tears trickled down their cheeks. The baron repeatedly embraced Candide, calling him his brother and deliverer.

'Perhaps, dear Candide,' he said, 'we shall enter the city together as victors, and recover my sister.'

'That is all that I desire; for I intended to marry her, and still hope to do so.'

'What, insolent fellow! You would have the impudence to marry my sister, who has seventy-two quarterings! Really you have an assurance, even to speak to me of such an audacious design!'

Candide was thunderstruck. 'Reverend Father,' he said, 'what are all the quarterings in the world? I have delivered your sister from the clutches of a Jew and an Inquisitor. She is grateful to me, and wishes to marry me. Master Pangloss always told me that all men are equal. I shall marry her, depend upon it!'

'We shall see about that, villain!' said the Jesuit Baron von Thunder-ten-Tronckh, and struck Candide across the face with the flat of his sword. Candide also drew, and plunged his sword up to the hilt in the Jesuit's belly. Then, pulling it out reeking hot, he burst into tears. 'O God!' he said, 'I have killed my old master, my friend, my brother-in-law. I am the mildest man in the world, yet I have already killed three men—and two of them were priests.'

Cacambo, who was standing guard at the gate of the arbour, came to see what had happened. 'Nothing remains to us but to sell our lives dear', said his master. 'Someone is bound to enter the arbour soon. We must die sword in hand.' But Cacambo had been in many such scrapes before, and kept calm. In a few seconds he stripped the Baron of his Jesuit's habit, put it on Candide, gave him the dead man's three-cornered hat, and made him mount.

'Gallop, master!' he said. 'Everybody will take you for a Jesuit on a tour of inspection. We shall have passed the frontier before they even start after us.' He rode rapidly ahead, shouting in Spanish: 'Make way, make way for the Reverend Father Colonel!'

CHAPTER XVI

THE GIRLS AND THE MONKEYS

By the time the German Jesuit's death was known in the camp, Candide and his valet were beyond the barriers. Cacambo had providently filled his wallet with bread, chocolate, ham, fruit and a few bottles of wine.

They rode on into an unexplored and pathless region, until they came to a beautiful meadow cut across by streams. Here they set their horses to graze. Cacambo advised his master to eat, and did so himself. 'How can you desire me to eat ham,' said Candide, 'when I have killed his lordship's son, and am doomed never to see Cunégonde again? What will it avail me to drag out a wretched existence, far from her, in remorse and despair? And what will the *Journal de Trevoux*[1] say?' Nevertheless, he ate.

The sun was now setting. The wanderers heard some faint cries, which seemed to have been uttered by women. They could not make out if these were cries of grief or of joy; but they rose hastily to their feet, with the disquiet that is caused by any unexpected event in an unknown country.

The cries, they now perceived, came from two young women, who were running nimbly along the edge of the meadow, pursued by two monkeys, which were biting their buttocks. Candide had learnt musketry with the Bulgarians, and could hit a filbert in a hedge without touching a leaf. He picked up his double-barrelled Spanish musket and killed both monkeys. 'God be praised, my dear Cacambo,' he said, 'I have rescued these two poor creatures from a grave peril. If it was a sin to kill an Inquisitor and a Jesuit, I have atoned for it by saving two girls' lives. Perhaps they are young ladies of good family, and this adventure may be of great service to us in this country.'

He was suddenly silenced by the sight of the two girls, who were affectionately embracing the dead monkeys, weeping and lamenting. 'Really,' he said, 'I would never have expected so much Christian charity.'

'You have done a fine stroke there, master!' said Cacambo, 'You have killed these two ladies' lovers.'

'Their lovers! You are jesting, Cacambo.'

'My dear master, everything surprises you. Why do you think it strange that there should be a country where monkeys win ladies' favours? They are a fourth part men, as I am a fourth part Spaniard.'

'Indeed,' said Candide with a sigh, 'I remember my master Pangloss telling me that such freaks were common

[1] A celebrated literary review, edited by members of the Society of Jesus throughout the first half of the eighteenth century.

in former times, and that these conjunctions produced egipans, fauns and satyrs, which were actually seen by many of the ancients; but I took all these tales for fables.'

'Now you see that they were true—and you see how people behave if they have not received a certain education. But what I fear is that these ladies may do us some mischief.'

This prudent remark persuaded Candide to leave the meadow and plunge into a wood. He and Cacambo finished their supper, and then, cursing the Inquisitor, the Governor of Buenos Aires and the Baron, they went to sleep in the undergrowth.

When they awoke, they could not move. During the night the Oreillons—this was the name of the local tribe—had learnt of their presence from the two ladies, and had tied them up with ropes made of bark. They were now surrounded by about fifty naked Oreillons armed with bows and arrows, clubs and flint-headed axes. Some were bringing a large cauldron to the boil, whilst others prepared spits. 'A Jesuit, a Jesuit!' they shouted. 'We shall be revenged, and shall have a good meal. Let us eat the Jesuit, eat the Jesuit!'

'I told you, master,' said Cacambo, 'that those wenches would play a scurvy trick on us.'

'We are certainly about to be either boiled or roasted. Ah, what would Pangloss say to this example of the behaviour of natural man in his pure state? Everything is good, says he. That may be; but I confess that it is hard to have lost Mistress Cunégonde, and then to be impaled on a spit by the Oreillons.'

'Do not lose hope. I understand a little of the jargon of these people, and will speak to them.'

'Be sure you point out to them how inhuman it is to boil and roast one's fellow-men, and how much at variance with Christian teaching.'

'Gentlemen,' said Cacambo, 'you no doubt suppose that today you are going to eat a Jesuit. 'Tis very well: indeed, no manner of treating an enemy could be more appropriate. The law of nature teaches us: "Thou shalt kill thy neighbour"—and this teaching is followed all over the world. If we in Europe neglect our right also to eat him, it is because we have better fare. But you have not such resources as we; and certainly it is better to eat one's enemies than to abandon the fruits of victory to the ravens and carrion-crows.

'But, gentlemen, you would not wish to eat your friends. It is not a Jesuit whom you are planning to roast, but your defender, the enemy of your enemies. For myself, I was born in your country. This gentleman is my master, and so far from being a Jesuit, he has lately killed one, and is wearing the spoils taken from him. That is how you came to make your mistake.

'To confirm the truth of what I say, take his habit to the nearest barrier of the Jesuit kingdom, and inquire whether my master did not kill one of their officers. It will take you little time; and, if I have lied to you, you can always eat us later. But if I have told you the truth, you know too well the laws of society, humanity and justice not to show us clemency.'

The Oreillons thought this speech very reasonable. They deputed two of their leading men to go at once and learn the truth. These two performed their task intelligently, and soon returned with favourable news. The Oreillons unbound their captives, treated them with great courtesy, offering them women and refreshments, and led them to the frontier of their country, gaily shouting: 'He is no Jesuit, he is no Jesuit!'

'What men, what manners!' thought Candide. 'Had I not been so fortunate as to have run Cunégonde's brother through the body, I should inexorably have been eaten. But, after all, pure natural man has much to be said for him: these people showed me a thousand civilities, the moment they knew I was not a Jesuit.'

CHAPTER XVII

EL DORADO—1

'WELL,' said Cacambo to his master, when they were at the frontier of the Oreillons, 'as you see, this hemisphere is no better than the other. Take my advice, and let us return to Europe the shortest way.'

'But how, and whither? In my own country the Bulgarians and Abarians are laying all waste. If I return to Portugal, I shall be burnt. If we abide here, we are every moment in danger of being roasted on spits. But how can I bring myself to quit that part of the world which contains Mistress Cunégonde?'

'Let us make for Cayenne. We shall find Frenchmen there—they are everywhere—and they will be able to help us. Perhaps God will take pity on us.'

It was not easy to reach Cayenne. They knew more or less in which direction to travel, but the way was barred by mountains, rivers, precipices, brigands and savages. Their horses died of fatigue and their provisions ran out. For a month they lived on wild fruit.

At length they came to a stream bordered by coconut palms. The sight of these gave them new life and hope. Cacambo, who was as ready with advice as the old woman, said: 'We are exhausted, and can march no farther. I spy an empty canoe; let us fill it with coconuts, embark, and drift down with the current. A river always leads to some inhabited place. If we find nothing pleasant, at least we shall find something new.'

'Agreed. Let us place ourselves in the hands of Providence.'

For a few leagues they were wafted between banks that were sometimes flowery, sometimes barren, sometimes level, sometimes rugged. The river gradually widened, until it reached a point where it disappeared into a tunnel beneath huge, terrifying crags. They decided to risk entering the tunnel, although the river, which had narrowed at this point, carried them along with dreadful speed and noise.

Twenty-four hours later they again saw daylight; but just as they did so, their canoe was dashed to pieces on a reef. For a whole league they had to drag themselves from rock to rock. Then the ravine opened out upon an immense horizon, rimmed with inaccessible mountains.

The country appeared to be cultivated as much for beauty as for the production of crops. On the roads were many carriages, of lovely design and made of some glittering material, carrying men and women of remarkable good looks and drawn by big red sheep, which were faster than the best horses of Andalusia, Tetuan or Mequinez.

'Here is a country that beats Westphalia', said Candide. They struck up from the river bank towards the first village they saw. Some village children, dressed in tattered gold brocade, were playing quoits by the entrance. The two Europeans noticed with interest that the quoits were large round discs, yellow, red, and green, of remarkable brilliance. They were, in fact, lumps of gold, ruby and emerald. The travellers felt a strong desire to collect some of them: the smallest would have made the biggest ornament in the throne of the Great Mogul.

'These children must be the sons of the king of this country', said Cacambo. At this moment the village teacher came to call the children back to their lessons. 'There is the royal family's tutor', said Candide.

The urchins left their quoits, and a number of other toys

lying on the ground. Candide picked them up and respectfully handed them to the teacher, indicating by signs that their Royal Highnesses had forgotten their gold and jewels. The teacher smiled, threw the objects down, glanced at Candide in surprise and followed the children back to the school.

The travellers carefully collected the treasures. 'What a strange country!' said Candide. 'The royal children here must be very properly educated, since they are taught to despise gold and precious stones.'

They approached the first house in the village, which was built on the scale of a European palace. There was a crowd of people by the gate, and a greater number inside. Delightful music, and a savoury smell of cooking, came from the house. Cacambo went up to the gate, and heard the people talking Peruvian. This was his mother tongue—as was previously mentioned, he was born in Tucuman, and in his native village only Peruvian was spoken.

'I will be your interpreter', he told Candide. 'This is an inn, let us enter.'

Two waiters and two maids, all dressed in cloth of gold and wearing ribbons in their hair, invited them to sit down to the ordinary. Dinner consisted of four different soups, each garnished with two parrots, a boiled condor weighing two hundred pounds, two roasted monkeys of excellent flavour, three hundred humming-birds in one dish and six hundred fly-catchers in another, and a number of delicious ragoûts and tarts. The whole meal was served in dishes of a kind of rock-crystal. The servants passed around liquors of various kinds, extracted from the sugar-cane.

Most of the company were pedlars and waggoners. They all had excellent manners: they asked Cacambo a few circumspect questions, and answered his questions willingly and fully.

After dinner Candide and Cacambo deposited on the table two of the big gold pieces that they had picked up, thinking that these would amply pay for their meal. The landlord and landlady burst out laughing. 'We can see that you are strangers here, gentlemen', said the landlord. 'We are not accustomed to such, so you must pardon us for laughing when you offer to pay us with stones off the high-road. No doubt you are not supplied with coin of this realm; but you need none, to dine here. All inns established for the convenience of merchants are paid for by the government. You have dined ill here, because this is a poor village; but everywhere else you will be received fittingly.'

Cacambo translated the gist of all this to Candide, whose surprise and bewilderment were as great as his valet's. 'What sort of a country is this,' said Cacambo, 'cut off from all the rest of the world, where nothing happens as it does amongst us?'

'Probably this is the country where everything is good—for there must be such a country somewhere; and, whatever Pangloss may have said, I often perceived that by no means everything was good in Westphalia.'

CHAPTER XVIII

EL DORADO—2

CACAMBO kept plying the landlord with questions, until the latter remarked: 'I am a most ignorant man, and content to remain so. But we have here an old man, a former servant of the court, who is more learned, and also more communicative, than anyone else in the kingdom.' He led Cacambo—accompanied by Candide, who was content to play a secondary part, as his valet's companion—to the old man's house.

It was a very modest dwelling, the door being made only

of silver, and the wainscoting only of gold; but both were so elegantly wrought as to bear comparison with the most sumptuous. The ante-chamber was a plain affair of rubies and emeralds; but here, too, good taste atoned for extreme simplicity.

The old man seated his visitors on a sofa stuffed with humming-birds' feathers, had drinks brought to them in diamond goblets, and proceeded to satisfy their curiosity.

'I am one hundred and seventy-two years old,' he said, 'and my late father, who was equerry to the King, told me of the amazing revolutions that he had witnessed in Peru. The kingdom in which you find yourselves is the ancient country of the Incas, who very imprudently sallied from it to conquer another part of the world, and were themselves in the end destroyed by the Spaniards.

'Some of the royal princes were wiser than the others, and remained in their native country. With the people's consent they made a law that no inhabitant of our little kingdom should ever leave it. To this we owe the preservation of our innocence and happiness.

'The Spaniards had some confused knowledge of this country, which they called El Dorado; and an Englishman, a knight named Raleigh, actually came very near it about a hundred years ago. But the unscalable rocks and precipices by which we are surrounded have always hitherto sheltered us from the rapacity of the European nations, who have an unaccountable fondness for the pebbles and dirt of our land, for the sake of which they would kill us all to the last man.'

A long conversation followed, concerning the country's form of government, its customs, women, public spectacles and arts. Candide, with his taste for metaphysics, inquired through Cacambo if the country had a religion.

The old man reddened a little. 'Can you doubt it?' he said. 'Do you take us for ingrates?'

Cacambo respectfully asked what was the religion of El Dorado, and the old man grew redder. 'Can there be two religions, then? We have, so I suppose, the same religion as the rest of the world. We worship God from morning till night.'

'Do you worship a single God?' asked Cacambo, still acting as Candide's interpreter.

'Certainly. There are not two, three or four Gods. I must confess that the people of your world ask most singular questions.'

Candide, however, persisted with his interrogation. He asked in what manner people prayed in El Dorado.

'We do not pray at all. We have nothing to ask of God. He has given us all we want, and we unceasingly give Him thanks.'

Candide next inquired where could he find the priests of this religion. The old man smiled: 'My friends,' he said, 'we are all priests. The King and all the heads of families sing hymns of thanksgiving each morning, accompanied by five or six thousand musicians.'

'Then have you no monks among you, to teach, dispute, govern, intrigue, and burn people who disagree with them?'

'Do you take us for madmen? There is no disagreement among us; and I do not know what you mean by monks.'

Candide was delighted. 'This is very different from Westphalia,' he thought, 'and also from his lordship's castle. If friend Pangloss had ever seen El Dorado he would never have said that the castle of Thunder-ten-Tronckh was the finest thing on earth. There is nothing like seeing the world, that's certain.'

At the end of the conversation the old man put at the travellers' disposal a coach drawn by six sheep, with twelve of his servants, to conduct them to court. 'Excuse me,' he said, 'that my age deprives me of the honour of accompanying you. The King will receive you in a manner with which you will have no fault to find. If certain of the customs of the country do not please you, no doubt you will make allowances.'

The six sheep drew them at a great pace, and in less than four hours Candide and Cacambo arrived at the royal palace, which was on the outskirts of the capital. The portal was two hundred and twenty feet high and a hundred feet wide. It is impossible to describe the material of which it was made; it may be imagined, however, that it was far superior to the pebbles and sand which in Europe are called gold and jewels.

On leaving the coach, Candide and Cacambo were received by twenty beautiful maids-in-waiting, who conducted them to the baths and dressed them in garments made of the down of humming-birds. They were then led by high officials of both sexes to His Majesty's apartment. They passed between two rows of musicians, each numbering a thousand men, according to the local custom.

As they approached the presence chamber, Cacambo asked an official how they should salute His Majesty. Should they fall on their knees, or flat on their stomachs? Should they put their hands on their heads, or behind their backs? In short, what was the procedure?

'It is customary', said the official, 'to embrace the King, and to kiss him on both cheeks.' Candide and Cacambo did this, and were cordially welcomed by His Majesty, who invited them to sup with him.

In the meantime they were shown the city. The public buildings seemed almost to touch the clouds. The market places were adorned with thousands of columns. Fountains of clear water, rose-water and liquors drawn from the sugar-cane played incessantly in the squares, which were paved with jewels that gave off an odour like that of cloves and cinnamon.

Candide asked to see the courts of justice and the parliament. He learnt that there were no such things, and that there was no litigation in El Dorado. He asked if there were any prisons, and learnt that there were none. What surprised and pleased him still more was the Palace of the Sciences, where he saw a gallery two thousand yards long, filled with mathematical and scientific instruments.

In the course of the whole afternoon they saw perhaps a thousandth part of the city. They were then led back to the palace, where they sat down to table with His Majesty and several ladies. The dinner was excellent, and His Majesty a most entertaining host. Cacambo translated his jokes, which, as Candide noted with surprise, were witty even in translation.

They spent a month as the King's guests, and Candide began to get restive. 'I admit', he said to Cacambo, 'that the castle where I was born is nothing to this place. But, when all's said, Mistress Cunégonde is not here; and you, too, doubtless have some beloved one in Europe. If we remain here, we shall be only as the other inhabitants; whereas, if we return to our own world with but a dozen sheep laden with the pebbles of El Dorado, we shall be richer than all the kings of Europe, we shall have nothing to fear from the Inquisition, and we may easily recover Mistress Cunégonde.'

Cacambo agreed. The desire for freedom of movement, to cut a figure amongst their own people, and to tell their travellers' tales, induced these fortunate beings to forsake their good fortune. They asked His Majesty for leave to depart.

'You are acting foolishly', said the King. 'I know that my country is nothing very great. But when one is tolerably at ease in any place, he should remain there. I have, of course, no power to detain strangers: that would be an act of tyranny at variance both with our manner of life and with our code of law. All men are free—go when you will.

'But you will not find it easy. It is impossible to ascend the swift river by which you miraculously came, or to pass through the rocky tunnel. The mountains entirely surrounding my kingdom are ten thousand feet high, and as steep as walls. The passage from one side of them to the other is of more than ten leagues, and the descent on the far side is barred by precipices.

'However, since you are so set on leaving us, I will order the superintendents of machines to make one to help you on your journey. When you are beyond the crest, nobody can accompany you any farther; for my subjects have taken a vow never to pass beyond our frontier, and are too wise to break it. Anything else you ask, you shall have.'

'All we ask of Your Majesty', said Candide, 'is a few sheep laden with victuals, pebbles and the clay of your country.'

The King smiled: 'I cannot imagine what pleasure you Europeans find in our yellow clay. But take away as much as you will, and much good may it do you.'

On the King's orders, his engineers made a machine to hoist these two extraordinary men out of the kingdom. It took three thousand skilled engineers a fortnight to finish the work, which cost more than twenty million pounds sterling in the currency of the country. Candide and Cacambo were placed on the machine, together with two large red sheep saddled and bridled to carry them after they had crossed the mountains, twenty baggage sheep laden with victuals, thirty carrying gifts of rich native workmanship, and fifty laden with gold, diamonds and other jewels.

When they and their sheep had been ingeniously hoisted to the summit of the mountains, the engineers took leave of them. Candide was filled with the thought of presenting his sheep to Cunégonde. 'Now we have wherewithal to

pay the Governor of Buenos Aires,' he said, 'if Mistress
Cunégonde is to be had at any price whatsoever. Let us
make for Cayenne, and take ship there. Then let us see
what kingdom we shall purchase.'

CHAPTER XIX

THE DUTCH SHIPMASTER

THE first day's journey was pleasant, for the two travellers
were heartened by the thought that they possessed more
wealth than Asia, Europe and Africa put together. Deli-
ciously day-dreaming, Candide carved Cunégonde's name
on trees.

On the second day, two of their sheep were swallowed
up in swamps, with their loads. Two more died of fatigue
a few days later. Subsequently seven or eight starved to
death in a desert, and some others fell down precipices.
After a hundred days of travel they had only two sheep left.

'You see, my friend,' Candide remarked to Cacambo,
'how perishable are the riches of this world. Nothing lasts
but virtue, and the bliss of again seeing Mistress Cunégonde.'

'No doubt', said Cacambo. 'But we have still two sheep
left, with more treasure than ever the King of Spain will
own; and yonder I see a city which I take to be Surinam, a
colony of the Dutch. We are at the end of our troubles, and
the beginning of our pleasures.'

Near the city they found a negro lying on the ground.
He wore only a pair of blue linen breeches, and his left leg
and right hand had been cut off. 'My God,' said Candide in
Dutch, 'what dost thou here, friend, in this deplorable
condition?'

'I am waiting for my master, Mynheer Vanderendur, the
great merchant', said the negro.

'Was it he that used you thus?'

'Yes, sir; it is the custom here. They give us a pair of linen breeches twice a year, and that is all our covering. When we labour in the sugar-works, and the mill catches a finger, they cut off a hand. When we try to run away, they cut off a leg. I have suffered both these misfortunes. This is the price at which you eat sugar in Europe.

'But 'tis strange to think that, when my mother sold me for ten pattacoons on the Guinea coast, she said to me: "Dear child, bless our Fetishes and adore them always. They will make you live happily. You have the honour to be the slave of our lords the whites, and you are making the fortune of your father and mother." Alas, I know not whether I have made their fortune; but they have not made mine. Dogs, monkeys and parrots are a thousand times less wretched than the like of us. The Dutch Fetishes who converted me tell us every Sunday that all men, blacks and whites, are the children of Adam. I know nothing of genealogies; but, if what these preachers say be true, we are all first cousins—and you must allow that no one could treat relations more horribly.'

'Ah, Pangloss!' Candide exclaimed, 'you never guessed at such an abomination! This is the end. I must renounce your optimism.'

'Optimism,' said Cacambo, 'what is that?'

'It is the madness of asserting that everything is good, when it is evil.' Candide looked again at the negro, and burst into tears: thus, weeping, he entered Surinam.

They at once inquired if there were a vessel in the harbour which would put in to Buenos Aires. The person they spoke to happened to be a Spanish shipmaster, who offered them reasonable terms, and made an appointment with them at an inn. Candide and Cacambo went there to wait for him, taking with them their two sheep.

When they met, Candide, who always blurted out whatever was foremost in his mind, told the Spaniard all his adventures and disclosed his intention of carrying off Mistress Cunégonde.

'In that case, I would not dream of carrying you to Buenos Aires', said the shipmaster. 'I should be hanged, and so should you. The fair Cunégonde is the Governor's favourite mistress.'

Candide was aghast at this news, and wept for a long time. Then he took Cacambo aside. 'I'll tell you what you must do, my dear friend', he said. 'Each of us has in his pockets diamonds to the value of five or six millions. You are more clever than I. Go to Buenos Aires and bring off Mistress Cunégonde. If the Governor makes any difficulty, give him a million. If he holds out, give him two. You have not killed an Inquisitor, so they have nothing against you.

'For my part, I'll fit out another ship and go to Venice, where I will wait for you. Venice is a free country, where we shall have nothing to fear from Bulgarians or Abarians, Jews or Inquisitors.'

Cacambo thoroughly agreed with this proposal. He was unhappy at parting from a good master, who had become his close friend; but the pleasure of doing him a service outweighed the grief of leaving him. He set out the same day, having been reminded by Candide not to forget the old woman. Cacambo was a very good man.

Candide remained some time longer in Surinam, waiting for another captain to carry him and his two remaining sheep to Italy. He engaged servants, and bought all that he needed for a long voyage. At length the merchant Mynheer Vanderendur, who was master of a large vessel, offered his services.

'What will you take', said Candide, 'to carry me, my servants, my baggage and these two sheep directly to

Venice?' The shipmaster asked ten thousand piastres, and Candide immediately agreed.

'Ho, ho!' thought Vanderendur, 'this foreigner must be very rich.' A little while later, he came back and said that he could not sail for less than twenty thousand. 'Very well, you shall have them', said Candide.

'Zounds!' muttered the shipmaster. Coming back a second time, he raised his price to thirty thousand piastres. 'You shall have them', said Candide.

'Ho, ho!' again thought the Dutchman, 'thirty thousand piastres are nothing to this man. Those sheep must certainly be laden with an immense treasure. I'll ask no more at present, but make him first pay the thirty thousand, and then we shall see.'

Candide sold two small diamonds, the smaller of which was worth all the money that the shipmaster demanded, and paid him in advance. The two sheep were put on board, and Candide took a small boat to join the ship in the roads. The shipmaster seized his opportunity, hoisted his sails, and put to sea with a favourable wind.

Bewildered and stupefied, Candide soon lost sight of the ship. 'Alas,' he exclaimed, 'this is a trick worthy of the world to which I am returning.' Crushed with grief, he put back to the shore, having lost the wealth of twenty monarchs.

His next act was to visit the Dutch magistrate. Being somewhat agitated, he banged violently on the door, and in stating his case spoke a little louder than was necessary. The magistrate fined him ten thousand piastres for making so much noise: after which he listened patiently, promised to look into the matter as soon as the merchant returned, and charged another ten thousand piastres for the costs of the hearing.

This behaviour reduced Candide to utter desperation. He

had in his lifetime suffered far worse misfortunes than this; but the cool impudence of the magistrate, coming on top of the villainy of the shipmaster, inflamed his choler and plunged him in a black melancholy. The wickedness of mankind presented itself nakedly before him, and he became obsessed with gloomy thoughts.

Shortly afterwards he learnt that a French ship was about to sail for Bordeaux. As he had no more sheep laden with diamonds, he hired a cabin at a reasonable price. He also advertised in the town that he would pay passage, board, and two thousand piastres to any honest man who would accompany him on the voyage; a condition being, that this man must be the most unfortunate, and the most dissatisfied with his lot, in the whole province.

The crowd of candidates who presented themselves was larger than a whole fleet could carry. Seeking to narrow the field of choice, Candide selected about twenty men who seemed congenial, and invited them to dine with him at his inn. He stipulated that each of them should undertake to give a true account of his life; whilst Candide, for his part, promised to choose as his companion the man who should seem to him the most deserving of compassion, and the most justly dissatisfied with his lot. He also promised to give each of the others a small present.

The session lasted until four in the morning. Candide was reminded of what the old woman had said on the voyage to Buenos Aires, when she wagered that every single person on board the ship had suffered great misfortunes. As each story was told, he thought to himself: 'Pangloss would be hard put to it now to maintain his favourite thesis. For sure, if everything is good, it can only be in El Dorado, and nowhere else on earth.'

Candide finally decided in favour of a poor scholar who had worked for ten years for the book publishers of

Amsterdam—no employment, he reflected, could be more disgusting than this. This scholar (who was, as it happened, a very good sort of man) had been robbed by his wife, beaten by his son and forsaken by his daughter, who had eloped with a Portuguese. He had lost the small employment by which he lived, and was being persecuted by the clergy of Surinam, who thought that he was a Socinian.

It must be admitted that all the other candidates were at least as unfortunate as this one. Candide's real reason for choosing him was a hope that, being a well-read man, he would relieve the tedium of the voyage. The other candidates all thought that Candide was doing them an injustice; but he appeased them by giving each a thousand piastres.

CHAPTER XX

MARTIN THE MANICHÆAN

CANDIDE and the old scholar, whose name was Martin, had both of them seen and suffered so much that even if the ship had been sailing from Surinam to Japan, *via* the Cape of Good Hope, the subject of moral and physical evil could have kept them busy talking throughout the voyage.

Candide, however, had one great advantage over Martin: he still hoped to see Cunégonde again, whereas Martin had nothing to look forward to. Moreover, Candide had money and jewels. True, he had lost eighty red sheep laden with the world's greatest treasure, and he was still vexed by the roguery of the Dutch shipmaster: nevertheless, when he thought of what he still had in his pockets, or spoke of Cunégonde—and especially after a good dinner— he continued to incline towards the doctrines of Pangloss.

'Tell me, Mr. Martin,' he said, 'what is your opinion of the whole matter? What notion have you of moral and physical evil?'

'Sir, the clergy have accused me of being a Socinian. But the truth is, I am a Manichæan.'

'Surely you are jesting. There are no Manichæans left in these times.'

'There is myself. I cannot help it. I can hold no other belief.'

'The devil must be in you, then.'

'Perhaps he is. He interferes so much in the world's affairs, he might as well be in my body as everywhere else. I confess that, when I contemplate this globe, or rather globule, I believe that God has handed it over—excepting always El Dorado—to some malignant being.

'I have seen scarcely a city that did not wish the ruin of its neighbouring city; nor a family that did not wish to exterminate some other family. Everywhere the weak hate the powerful, before whom they crawl, and the powerful treat the weak like sheep, selling their wool and their carcases.

'A million regimented assassins scour Europe, earning their livelihoods by authorized murder and brigandage, because this is regarded as the most glorious of trades.

'Even in cities that seem to be at peace, where the arts flourish, men are eaten up with envy, cares and disquiets worse than the sufferings of a town under siege. Secret chagrins are even more bitter than public calamities.

'In short, I have seen and experienced so much that I am a Manichæan.'

'Yet there is some good in the world.'

'May be so, but it has never come to my notice.'

This discussion was interrupted by the sound of gunfire, which grew louder. Taking out their glasses, they saw two ships fighting, about three miles away. The wind carried both ships so near to the French vessel that those on board the latter had the pleasure of watching the engagement in comfort. It ended when one of the ships sent the other to the bottom with a low and accurately aimed broadside. Candide and Martin could plainly see a hundred men gesticulating and shrieking on the deck of the sinking ship. A moment later, all were swallowed up.

'Well,' said Martin, 'you see how men treat one another.'

''Tis true, there is something diabolical in this business.'

As Candide spoke, he saw a brilliant red object floating close to their ship. The longboat was hoisted out, to discover what it was. It was one of his sheep. Candide felt more joy at the recovery of this one animal than he had felt grief at losing eighty of them, all laden with the treasures of El Dorado.

The French captain told them that the victorious ship was a Spaniard, and the other a Dutch pirate. Its skipper was, in fact, the very man who had robbed Candide. The immense riches which the scoundrel had thus acquired were now sunk with him in the sea.

'You see', said Candide, 'that crime is sometimes punished. That rascal of a Dutch skipper has met the fate he deserved.'

'Yes, but why should the passengers on his ship also perish? God may have punished the rogue, but the devil drowned the rest.'

The French and Spanish ships continued their cruise, and Candide and Martin continued their discussions. They argued for a fortnight, at the end of which they were as far advanced as at the beginning. However, the main thing was that they conversed, and in the exchange of ideas found consolation for their griefs.

Candide frequently embraced his sheep. 'Since I have found thee again,' he said to it, 'I may well find Cunégonde also.'

CHAPTER XXI

THE NATURE OF MANKIND

'WERE you ever in France, Mr. Martin?' asked Candide. They were within sight of the coast.

'Yes, I have passed through several of her provinces. In some, the half of the inhabitants are mad; in others, they are too artful; in others, they are mostly rather simple and stupid; in still others, they affect to be witty. In all of them, however, the chief occupation is making love, the second is slander, and the third is talking nonsense.'

'But have you seen Paris, Mr. Martin?'

'Yes, I have been there. It contains all the kinds I have mentioned. It is a chaos, a throng, where everyone seeks for pleasure, and, as far as I could make out, scarcely anyone finds it.

'On my arrival there, I had all my money stolen by pickpockets at the fair of Saint Germain. I myself was arrested as a thief, and imprisoned for a week. Afterwards I worked as a publisher's proof-reader, to earn enough to return to Holland on foot. I came to know the whole pack of scribblers, caballers and religious jumping-jacks.[1] Some of the people are said to be very polite. I would like to believe it.'

'For my part,' said Candide, 'I have no wish to see France. As you may well imagine, after spending a month in El Dorado there is nothing else on earth that I wish to see—excepting Mistress Cunégonde. I am going to wait

[1] In French, '*la canaille convulsionnaire*'. '*Convulsionnaires*' was the name given in the reign of Louis XV to a group of Jansenists who on occasion would go into fits of religious ecstasy similar to those of the negro 'holy rollers' of modern times.

for her at Venice, and will pass through France on my way to Italy. Will you not go with me?'

'Gladly. I have heard that life in Venice is pleasant only for the rich, but that visitors who have plenty of money are very well received there. I have none, but you have; so I shall follow you whither you please.'

'While we are on the subject, do you believe that the earth was originally sea, as is stated in that great book that belongs to the captain?'

'I believe nothing of the sort, any more than I do all the other fancies that have been foisted upon us through the centuries.'

'But to what end, think you, was the world formed?'

'To turn our brains.'

'Were you not astonished by that story I told you, of the two girls in the country of the Oreillons, who had monkeys for lovers?'

'Not in the least. I see nothing strange in such an infatuation. I have seen so many extraordinary things that now nothing is extraordinary to me.'

'Do you think that men always slaughtered one another, as they do nowadays? Were there always liars, cheats, traitors, brigands, weaklings, deceivers, cowards, enviers, gluttons, drunkards, misers, sycophants, butchers, slanderers, debauchees, fanatics, hypocrites and fools?'

'Do you think that hawks have always devoured pigeons at every opportunity?'

'Doubtless.'

'Well, then, if hawks have always been the same, why should men have been altered?'

'Ah, but there is a great difference, for Free Will . . .'

They were still arguing when they arrived at Bordeaux.

CHAPTER XXII

A RICH STRANGER IN PARIS

CANDIDE stayed in Bordeaux only long enough to sell a few of the pebbles of El Dorado, and to procure a good chaise with room for two people. He now found the philosopher Martin's company indispensable. He was distressed, however, at having to part with his sheep, which he gave to the Bordeaux Academy of the Sciences. The Academy proposed as the theme for its yearly prize competition an investigation into the reason for the redness of the sheep's wool. The prize was won by a scholar from the north, who demonstrated by $\frac{A + B - C}{Z}$ that the sheep must of necessity be red, and furthermore that it would die of the rot.

It struck Candide that all the travellers whom he met at inns along the road told him that they were going to Paris. This general eagerness to go there at length made him wish to see the city, which was not much out of the way to Venice.

He entered by the Faubourg St. Marceau, which was like one of the worst villages in Westphalia. On putting up at an inn, he was overtaken by a slight illness, caused by fatigue. Since he wore a huge diamond on one of his fingers, and had in his carriage a weighty strong-box, he was attended by two physicians, whom he had not asked for, by a number of close friends who were always by his bedside, and by two devoted females, who kept ordering cups of broth for him.

'I, too, have been ill in Paris,' said Martin, 'but I was

very poor, and had no friends, nurses or physicians. I recovered.'

As a result of purgings and bleedings, Candide's illness became serious. A priest of the parish came and offered to sell him a note of exchange, payable to the bearer in the other world.[1] Candide refused the transaction, although the two females assured him that it was the latest fashion. Candide told them that he was not a man of fashion, and Martin offered to throw the priest out of the window. The priest swore that Candide would not receive burial, and Martin swore that it was he who would bury the priest, if he continued to plague them. After a heated argument, Martin took the priest by the shoulders and turned him out of the room: this caused a great scandal, and information was laid against Candide with the authorities.

Candide recovered. During his convalescence a number of his attentive companions regularly came and dined with him. They played cards, for high stakes. Candide was surprised to find that he never held any aces: this did not surprise Martin.

Amongst Candide's visitors was a little abbé from Perigord, one of those obsequious, quick-witted, obliging, impudent, fawning, useful creatures who lie in wait for passing strangers, tell them the scandal of the town, and offer them pleasures at various prices. This abbé took Candide and Martin to the *Comédie*, where a new tragedy was being performed.

Candide's seat was next to a party of wits; but this did not prevent him from weeping at some moving and beautifully acted scenes. During an interval, one of the talkative bores who had been sitting near by remarked to him: 'You

---

[1] An allusion to the '*billets de confession*', which in Voltaire's time Catholic priests customarily demanded, before they would give the last sacrament.

should not have wept. That actress is wretched, and the actor who plays with her is even worse. The piece is worse than the actors. The author does not know a word of Arabic, yet he has laid his scene in Arabia. What is more, the fellow does not believe in innate ideas. Tomorrow I will bring you a score of pamphlets that have been written against him.'

Afterwards Candide asked the abbé how many theatrical pieces there were in France.

'Five or six thousand.'

''Tis a great number. How many of them are good?'

'Fifteen or sixteen.'

''Tis a great number.'

Candide was greatly taken with an actress who was one of the audience. She had made her name, so the abbé told him, by playing Queen Elizabeth in a rather dull tragedy that is still sometimes performed. 'I like that actress', said Candide. 'She has a deceiving resemblance to Mistress Cunégonde. I should be very glad to pay my respects to her.'

The abbé offered to introduce him to the actress at her house. Candide, having been brought up in Germany, wanted to know what was the etiquette, and how a stage Queen of England was treated in France.

'That depends on the circumstances', said the abbé. 'In a country town we take them to a tavern. Here in Paris they are treated with great respect while they are beautiful, and are thrown on a dunghill when they die.'

'A queen thrown on a dunghill!'

'Yes, the abbé is right', said Martin. 'I was in Paris when Mlle. Monime made her exit, as you may say, out of this world into another. She was refused what they call here "honours of sepulture", that is to say, she was denied the privilege of rotting in a mean churchyard with all the beggars of the parish. She was buried all by herself, at the corner of the Rue de Bourgogne; which must have shocked her extremely, as she had very exalted ideas.'

'That was far from polite', said Candide.

'What do you expect? These people are like that. Imagine to yourself all possible contradictions and inconsistencies: you will find them all in the government, the courts of justice, the churches and the public spectacles of this odd nation.'

'Is it true that Parisians are always laughing?'

'Yes,' said the abbé, 'but only in anger. They complain of everything with loud bursts of laughter. Even when themselves behaving in the most abominable manner, they laugh.'

'Who was that filthy great lout who spoke so ill of the piece that moved me so much, and of the players who gave me so much pleasure?'

'A good-for-nothing who gets his livelihood by abusing each book and play that appears. He hates everything successful as eunuchs hate great lovers. He is one of those literary vipers who feed on dirt and venom—a pamphleteer.'

'And what is that?'

'A hack journalist, a Fréron.'[1]

As they spoke, Candide, Martin and the abbé were standing on the main staircase of the theatre, watching the audience depart. 'Although my one wish is to see Mistress Cunégonde again,' said Candide, 'yet I should like to sup with Mlle. Clairon'—this was the name of the actress already mentioned—'for I much admired her.'

The abbé did not, in fact, dare to approach Mlle. Clairon, who was fastidious about the company she kept. 'She is engaged this evening,' he said, 'but I will do myself the honour to lead you to the house of a lady of quality, where

[1] Editor of the *Année littéraire*, and a bitter enemy of Voltaire.

you will come to know as much of Paris as if you had lived here for forty years.'

Candide, who was always eager for new experiences, agreed to visit the lady, who lived in the depths of the Faubourg St.-Honoré. The company was playing faro: a dozen gloomy punters held in front of them hands of cards—gloomy and preposterous registers of their misfortunes. There was a deep hush in the room; the punters were pale and the banker was tense.

The lady of the house sat by the banker and kept a lynx-like watch on the bidding, which consisted of mutters of 'double' or 'raise it seven times'. When one of the gamblers bent the corner of a card, she made him straighten it out. Her manner in so doing was strict, but polite: she showed no anger, so as not to frighten away her customers.

The name this lady went by was the Marquise de Paro-lignac. Her fifteen-year-old daughter was one of the punters, and made signs to her mother whenever one of the unfortunate gamesters tried to soften the rigours of chance by cheating.

When the abbé, Candide and Martin came in, nobody got up, greeted them or looked their way. 'My Lady Baroness of Thunder-ten-Tronckh would have behaved more civilly', thought Candide. The abbé whispered something to the marquise, who half raised herself from her chair and gave Candide a gracious smile and Martin a distant nod. She ordered a chair and a pack of cards to be fetched for Candide, who proceeded to lose fifty thousand francs in a few deals. After this the company had supper. Everyone marvelled at the calmness with which Candide bore his losses, and the lacqueys whispered that he must be an English milord.

The supper, like most suppers in Paris, opened in silence, which was followed first by a confused babble and then by the repetition of a number of jokes, mostly rather insipid, some inaccurate gossip, some pointless discussions, a little politics, and a great deal of scandal. There was even some talk about books. 'Has anyone read the new romance by the Doctor of Divinity, the Sieur Gauchat?'[1] the abbé asked the company.

'Yes,' replied one of the guests, 'but I had not the patience to go through with it. The town is pestered with a swarm of impertinent productions, but this of Dr. Gauchat's out-does them all. Indeed, I am so cursedly tired of reading so much vile stuff that I have taken refuge in faro.'

'But what say you to Archdeacon Trublet's *Miscellany*?'[2]

'What a tedious creature!' said Mme. de Parolignac. 'What pains he is at to tell you what everybody knows already, and how he labours some point that is scarcely worth making! How clumsily he picks the brains of others—for he has none of his own—and how he mangles what he has pilfered! The man makes me sick: but he shall do so no longer—a few pages of the archdeacon are quite enough.'

One of the guests, who happened to be a man of learning and taste, agreed with the marquise. The conversation turned to plays, and the marquise asked why was it that so many utterly unreadable plays were still being performed. The man of taste explained that a piece of almost no merit may nevertheless have some interesting quality. It was not sufficient, he commented, for the author merely to throw together two or three of those situations which, though found in every romance, never lose their fascination for the public. A great work must be novel without being far-fetched; frequently sublime, but always natural. The author must know the human heart, and how to make it speak; he

---

[1] Author of a work entitled *Lettres sur quelques écrits de ce temps*.

[2] His principal work, *Essais de littérature et de morale*, was published in 1736.

must be a poet, without letting any of his characters speak like poets; and he must be a master of his language, using it purely and harmoniously and not letting the rhyme interfere with the sense.

'Whoever fails to observe any one of these conditions,' he concluded, 'though he may gain public applause with one or two plays, will never be reckoned in the number of good authors. There are very few good plays. Some of those that are produced are idylls cast in the form of dialogue, frequently well written and in good verse. Others are political tracts, which send one to sleep, or amplifications of the obvious, which are merely repellent. Others again are the fancies of a madman, composed in an uncouth style, with lapses into inconsequence, long apostrophes to the deities—inserted, doubtless, because the author does not know how to address his fellow-men—false maxims and stuffed-up commonplaces.'

Candide had listened with admiring attention. He now leant over to the marquise—she had arranged that he should be seated next to her—and asked in a whisper who this excellent talker might be.

'He is a man of letters', said the marquise. 'He does not play, but the abbé sometimes brings him to sup with me. He is a great judge of plays and books. He has himself written a play that was hissed off the stage, and a book that has never been seen outside his publisher's shop—except for one copy that he sent to me with a dedicatory inscription.'

'A truly great man,' said Candide, 'a second Pangloss!' Then, addressing the gentleman himself: 'Sir,' he said, 'I take it that you are of opinion that everything is for the best both in the physical and in the moral world, and that everything must be as it is?'

'I, sir! I think no such thing. I consider that everything in this world is awry; that no one knows his rank, his office, nor what he does nor what he should do; and that, except at supper, which is a fairly cheerful function and tends to produce concord, our time is spent on idle quarrels: Jansenists against Molinists, parliament against church, country against country, financiers against the people, women against their husbands, relations against relations. 'Tis a perpetual battlefield.'

'I have seen worse things than those you mention', said Candide. 'Yet a learned man, who has since had the misfortune to be hanged, taught me that everything was marvellously well, and that these evils are mere shadows in a beautiful picture.'

'Your gallows-bird was laughing at you', said Martin. 'These shadows, as you call them, are horrible blemishes.'

''Tis not men who make these blemishes; they cannot act otherwise than as they do.'

'Then it is not their fault.'

Most of the gamesters did not understand a word of all this, and were busy drinking. Martin continued the discussion with the man of letters, whilst Candide told the lady of the house some of his adventures.

After supper the marquise took Candide to her boudoir, where she sat him on a sofa. 'Well,' she said, 'are you still so violently fond of Mistress Cunégonde von Thunderten-Tronckh?'

'Yes, madam.'

The marquise smiled affectionately. 'You answer like a young Westphalian. A Frenchman would have said: "It is true that I loved Mistress Cunégonde. But since I have seen you, I fear that I love her no longer."'

'Alas, madam, I will make what answer you please.'

'You fell in love with her, I am told, when you picked up her handkerchief. You shall pick up my garter.'

'Most willingly, madam.' Candide did so.

'But now you must tie it on again.' Candide did this too.

'Look ye, young man, you are a stranger here. I make some of my Parisian lovers languish for me a whole fortnight; but I surrender to you the first night, because it is a patriotic obligation to show hospitality to a young man from Westphalia.'

Whilst speaking, the beauty noticed that the young foreigner was wearing two enormous diamonds. She praised them with such unaffected enthusiasm that they were soon transferred from Candide's fingers to hers.

As he went home with Martin and the abbé, Candide felt some remorse at having been unfaithful to Cunégonde. The abbé, too, was dissatisfied. He had received only a small share of the fifty thousand francs that Candide had lost at play—not to speak of the two diamonds—and he was planning how to turn his acquaintance with Candide to the greatest possible profit.

He began talking about Cunégonde, and Candide remarked that when he saw her again, he would humbly ask her pardon for his unfaithfulness. The abbé listened with courteous attention. He seemed to take a keen interest in everything that Candide said, did, or planned to do.

'And so, sir, you have an engagement at Venice?'

'Yes, Monsieur l'Abbé. I absolutely must find Mistress Cunégonde.' Carried away by the pleasure of talking of his beloved, Candide related, as he so often did, some of his adventures with that illustrious Westphalian damsel.

'I suppose', said the abbé, 'that Mistress Cunégonde has a great deal of wit, and writes charming letters?'

'Indeed, I have never received any from her. For you must remember that, having been driven out of the castle for my love of her, I could not write to her, and soon afterwards I learnt that she was dead. I then found her and lost her again, and now I have sent a messenger to her, near two thousand leagues from hence, and am waiting here for the answer.'

The abbé listened attentively, and seemed pensive. Soon afterwards he cordially embraced Candide and Martin, and left them.

Next morning Candide received the following letter:

'My dearest Lover, for the last week I have been in this city, confined by illness. I have learnt that you are here, and should fly to your arms, were I able to stir. I learnt of your arrival when I was at Bordeaux, where I have left the faithful Cacambo and the old woman. They will soon follow me. The Governor of Buenos Aires has taken everything from me but your heart. Come to me: your presence will either give me new life, or kill me with pleasure.'

Torn between joy at this charming and unexpected letter and grief at the news of Cunégonde's illness, Candide took his gold and diamonds and found a guide to lead Martin and himself to the hotel where she was lodging. When he entered her room, he trembled, his heart beat violently, and his voice quavered. He started to draw back the bed-curtains, and called for a light.

'Ah, beware of doing that, sir!' said the chambermaid. 'Mistress cannot bear the light.' She quickly pulled the curtains closed again.

'Dearest Cunégonde,' sobbed Candide, 'how are you faring? If you cannot see me, speak to me, at least.'

'She cannot speak', said the maid.

The lady put a plump hand outside the curtains. Candide wetted it with his tears, and then filled it with diamonds. He also laid a purse of gold on the chair by the bedside.

An officer entered the room, followed by the abbé and a squad of men. 'Are these the suspected foreigners?' he asked, and gave orders that they should be arrested and taken off to prison.

'Travellers are not treated in this manner in El Dorado', said Candide.

'I am more a Manichæan than ever', said Martin.

'But pray, officer, where are you going to carry us?'

'To a dungeon.'

Martin collected his wits and realized that the pretended Cunégonde, the abbé and the officer were all frauds, and that the officer could easily be got rid of. He enlightened Candide, and the latter, in his impatience to see the true Cunégonde, immediately offered the officer a bribe of three small diamonds, worth about three thousand pistoles each.

'Ah, sir,' said the man with the ivory tipstaff, 'had you committed ever so many crimes, you would still be the best man living. Three diamonds, worth several thousand pistoles, I'll be bound! Why, sir, so far from carrying you to jail, I would give my life for you.

'There are orders for the arrest of all foreigners, but leave it to me. I have a brother at Dieppe, in Normandy. I will conduct you thither, and if you have a diamond for him, he will take as much care of you as I myself should.'

'But why are they arresting foreigners?'

The abbé broke into the conversation: 'A poor devil of an Atrebatian listened to some foolish stories, which excited him to parricide.[1] It was a crime different from that of May 1610,[2] but similar to that of December 1594,[3] and, indeed, to many other crimes committed in various months and years by other poor devils who have listened to foolish stories.'

The officer explained what the abbé was talking about. 'The monsters!' Candide exclaimed. 'To think that such

---

[1] There was an attempted assassination of Louis XV on 5 January 1757.

[2] The assassination of Henri IV.

[3] An attempted assassination of Henri IV.

horrid deeds should be committed among a people that is always singing and dancing. How can I most quickly escape from this country, where monkeys give offence to tigers? For God's sake, officer, conduct me to Venice, where I am to wait for Mistress Cunégonde.'

'I cannot conduct you farther than the coast of Normandy', said the officer. He ordered Candide's and Martin's irons to be struck off, told his men that a mistake had been made, and dismissed them. He then brought Candide and Martin to Dieppe, where he left them to the care of his brother.

There was a small Dutch ship in the roads, and the officer's brother, whose devoted loyalty had been purchased for three more diamonds, put Candide and Martin aboard it. The ship was about to sail for Portsmouth, in England. This was not on the direct route to Venice, but Candide did not care. He felt that he had escaped from hell, and reckoned on resuming his journey to Venice at the first opportunity.

CHAPTER XXIII

'TO ENCOURAGE THE OTHERS'

'Ah, Pangloss, Pangloss—ah, Martin, Martin—ah, dearest Cunégonde—what sort of a world is this?' So sighed Candide, aboard the Dutch vessel.

'Something utterly mad and abominable', said Martin.

'You know England. Are they as mad there as in France?'

'It is another kind of madness. As you know, these two nations are at war for the sake of a few acres of snow up towards Canada, and are spending on this fine war of theirs more than all Canada is worth. To say exactly whether there are more people fit for strait-waistcoats in the one country than in the other, exceeds the limits of my imperfect capacity. All I know is that, in general, the people we are going to visit are of an atrabilious disposition.'

At Portsmouth the shore was crowded with people eagerly watching a big man[1] who was kneeling on the deck of a man-of-war, with a bandage over his eyes. In front of him stood four soldiers, each of whom phlegmatically fired three bullets into the big man's skull. The crowd then dispersed, with an air of satisfaction.

'What is all this?' said Candide. 'What demon has the mastery of the world?' He inquired who the big man was. 'An admiral', he was told.

'And why was this admiral killed?'

'Because he did not kill enough men himself. He fought an engagement with a French admiral, and it is thought that he did not sufficiently close with him.'

'But surely, then, the French admiral was as far from him as he was from the other?'

'That is undeniable. But in this country it is found requisite now and then to kill an admiral, in order to encourage the others.'

Candide was so shocked that he would not set foot on shore. He struck a bargain with the Dutch skipper—wondering whether the latter would rob him, like the Dutch skipper at Surinam—for a direct passage to Venice.

The ship was ready to sail in two days. They sailed along the coast of France and passed within sight of Lisbon, at which Candide shuddered. They passed through the straits into the Mediterranean, and arrived at Venice. 'God be praised!' said Candide, embracing Martin. 'Here I shall see Cunégonde again. I trust Cacambo as I trust myself. Everything is good, as good as could possibly be.'

[1] Admiral Byng, who was executed on 14 March 1757.

CHAPTER XXIV

PAQUETTE AND FRIAR GIROFLÉE

In Venice Candide looked for Cacambo at every inn and coffee-house, and among all the ladies of pleasure, but could not find him. He sent every day to inquire what ships had come in: still no news of Cacambo.

'What!' he said to Martin. 'Have I had time to travel from Surinam to Bordeaux, thence to Paris, to Dieppe, to Portsmouth, to sail along the coasts of Portugal and Spain and up the Mediterranean, to spend some months in Venice—and still Cunégonde is not arrived? All that I have found in her place has been a female trickster. Cunégonde is certainly dead, and I have nothing to do but to follow her.

'Alas, how much better it would have been to remain in the paradise of El Dorado, than to have returned to this cursed Europe! You are in the right, my dear Martin: all is misery and deceit in this wicked world.'

He fell into a black melancholy, and took no part in the *opera alla moda*, or in any other of the carnival festivities. Not one lady paid the least attention to him.

'Upon my word,' said Martin, 'you are very simple to imagine that a mestizo valet, with five or six millions in his pockets, would go to the end of the world in search of your mistress and bring her to you at Venice. If he finds her, he will keep her for himself. If he does not find her, he will take another. I advise you to forget your valet Cacambo, and your mistress, too.'

Martin was no comfort. Candide's melancholy grew, whilst Martin continued to demonstrate to him that there was very little virtue or happiness on earth—except possibly in El Dorado, where nobody could go.

One day Candide saw on the Piazza di San Marco a young Theatine friar, with a girl under his arm. The friar was clear complexioned, plump, bright-eyed and vigorous, with an assured manner and a bold and spirited mien and bearing. The girl, who was very pretty, was singing. Now and then she glanced lovingly at her Theatine, and pinched his chubby cheeks.

'You will allow', said Candide to Martin, 'that there, at least, are two happy people. Everywhere, hitherto—except in El Dorado—I have met only unfortunates. But as to this couple, I wager they are most happy creatures.'

'I wager they are not.'

'Well, we have only to ask them to dine with us, and you will see whether I am mistaken.'

Candide thereupon accosted the couple, and with a bow invited them to come to his inn and dine on macaroni, Lombard partridges and caviare, with Montepulciano, Lachryma Christi and Cyprian and Samian wines.

The Theatine accepted the invitation. The girl blushed and followed the friar unwillingly, repeatedly staring at Candide with an air of surprise and embarrassment, her eyes full of tears. When they reached the inn, the friar remained downstairs for a drink before dinner, whilst the others went to Candide's apartment. Here the girl said to him: 'How, Master Candide, do you not recognise Paquette?'

Candide had not hitherto looked at her closely, since he cared for no woman but Cunégonde. 'Ah, my poor child!' he now exclaimed, 'is it you? And was it you who reduced Dr. Pangloss to that fine condition in which I saw him?'

'Alas, yes, sir, it is I, indeed, and I see that you know everything. I have learnt of the dreadful misfortunes that befel the whole household of her ladyship the Baroness and Mistress Cunégonde. I vow to you that my own lot has been scarcely less pitiful.

'I was a good girl when you saw me last. I was seduced by a Franciscan friar, who was my confessor: the consequences proved terrible. I was obliged to leave the castle, only a little while after the Baron kicked you out. If a famous surgeon had not taken compassion on me, I had been a dead woman. Out of gratitude, I lived with him for some time as his mistress. His wife, who was ragingly jealous, beat me unmercifully every day. She was a fury! The doctor was the ugliest man alive, and surely I was the unhappiest of all creatures, to be continually beaten for a man whom I did not love.

'You know, sir, how dangerous it is for a cross-grained woman to be married to a doctor. Incensed at his wife's behaviour, he took his opportunity one day when she had a slight cold, and gave her a medicine so efficacious that she died within two hours, in frightful convulsions.

'Her relations brought a criminal action against the doctor, who fled. I was put in jail. My innocence would not have saved me, had I not been tolerably handsome. The judge set me free, on condition that he should succeed the doctor. But I was soon supplanted by a rival, turned off without a farthing, and obliged to take to the abominable trade which you men think so pleasing, but which to us is nothing but a bottomless pit of misery.

'I came to exercise the profession at Venice. Ah, sir, did you but know what it is to be obliged to lie with every fellow—with old tradesmen, councillors, monks, gondoliers, abbés; to be exposed to all their insults and outrages; to be often reduced to borrowing a petticoat, only that it may be lifted by some disgusting man; to be robbed by one man of what one has earned from another; to have to pay bribes to officers of justice; and to have no other prospect than a hideous old age, ending in a hospital or on a dunghill: did you but know all this, you would conclude that I am one of the most unhappy creatures alive.'

'You see,' said Martin, 'I have won half of my wager already.'

'But you seemed so gay and content when I met you', Candide said to Paquette. 'You sang, you caressed the Theatine with an air of such genuine fondness, that I thought you to be as happy as—so it now appears—you are in truth wretched.'

'Ah, sir, that is one of the miseries of the trade. Yesterday I was beaten and robbed by an officer: and today I must seem merry to please a monk.'

Candide had heard enough; he admitted that Martin had won his wager—at least, as far as Paquette was concerned. They went to join the friar for dinner.

The meal was a pleasant one, and towards the end they were talking freely. 'Father,' said Candide, 'you seem a most enviable man. Your face glows with health and happiness, you have a pretty wench to divert you, and you seem very content to be a friar.'

'Faith, sir,' said Friar Giroflée, 'I could wish all Theatines at the bottom of the sea. I have been tempted a thousand times to set fire to the monastery and turn Turk.

'My parents obliged me, at the age of fifteen, to put on this detestable habit, so that they might leave a greater inheritance to an accursed elder brother, whom God confound!

'Our monastery is full of jealousy, discord and fury. I get a little money by preaching a few paltry sermons: the Prior robs me of the half of it, but the remainder pays for wenches. Yet, when I return to the monastery at night, I am ready to dash my head against the walls of the dormitory: and all the rest of the brotherhood are in like case.'

'Well,' said Martin, 'I think I have now won the wager entirely.'

Candide gave two thousand piastres to Paquette and a thousand to the friar. 'My answer is,' he said, 'that now, with this money, they will be happy.'

'I don't believe it. Perhaps these piastres will make them more wretched still.'

'Be that as it may, one thing comforts me. I see that one often meets people whom one had never expected to meet again. I have found my red sheep, and Paquette. It may well be that I shall also find Cunégonde.'

'Indeed, I wish that one day she may bring you happiness: but I much doubt it.'

'You are very harsh.'

'I have seen the world.'

'But observe these gondoliers. Are they not always singing?'

'You do not see them at home with their wives and brats. The Doge has his griefs—gondoliers have theirs. It is true that, in the main, a gondolier's lot is preferable to that of a doge: but the difference is so trifling that it is not worth the trouble of inquiring into.'

'There is talk of a certain Senator Pococurante, who lives in that fine house on the Brenta, and is hospitable to foreigners. He is said to be a man who has never known grief.'

'I should be glad to meet so extraordinary a being.'

Candide thereupon sent a message to Senator Pococurante, asking for permission to visit him next day.

CHAPTER XXV

SENATOR POCOCURANTE

CANDIDE and Martin took a gondola to Senator Pococurante's palace on the Brenta. Its gardens were extensive and adorned with fine marble statues, and the palace itself was of great beauty. The master of the house, a man of about sixty, and very rich, received the two sightseers civilly, but without much ceremony. Candide was disconcerted by this, but Martin was rather pleased.

Two pretty girls in neat dresses brought chocolate, which they stirred into a creamy froth. Candide remarked on their good looks and smart service.

'They are good enough creatures', said the senator. 'I make them lie with me sometimes, for I am heartily tired of the city ladies, their coquetry, their jealousy, their quarrels, their humours, their meannesses, their pride and their follies. I am tired of making sonnets, or of paying for sonnets to be made, in their honour.

'But now, after all, these girls begin to tax my patience.'

After breakfast they walked along a large gallery. Candide admired the pictures. Pausing by the first two they came to, he asked who had painted them. 'They are by Raphael', said the senator. 'I bought them, at a great price, seven years ago, purely from vanity, as they are said to be the finest pieces in Italy. They do not please me: the colours are gloomy, the figures do not come out enough, they want relief, and the draperies do not at all resemble any true stuff. In short, whatever may be said of them, they are not, in my opinion, a true representation of nature. I shall never like a picture, unless it makes me believe that I am beholding Nature herself: and there are no such pictures. I have many, but I no longer look at them.'

Before dinner Pococurante ordered music. Candide thought it delightful. 'This noise', said Pococurante, 'may entertain one for half an hour, but if it lasts longer it becomes tiresome to everybody, although no one dares to own it. Music in these days is no more than the art of performing the difficult; and that which is merely difficult, and nothing else, cannot please for long.

'I believe I might take more pleasure in opera, if they had

not found a way to turn it into a repulsive monstrosity. These wretched tragedies set to music—see them who will: where the scenes are contrived for no other purpose than to introduce, most incongruously, two or three songs designed to give some actress an opportunity of showing the powers of her gullet. Let who will, or can, swoon with pleasure to see a eunuch trilling and strutting his way through the part of Cæsar or Cato. For my part, I have long since forsaken these paltry spectacles, which constitute the glory of our modern Italy—and for which monarchs pay so dear.'

Candide argued against these sentiments, but only a little and with discretion. Martin was in full agreement with them.

After an excellent dinner, they repaired to the library, where Candide noticed a magnificently bound Homer. He complimented the senator on the possession of this treasure. 'This book', he said, 'was once the delight of the great Pangloss, the best philosopher in Germany.'

'It is no delight to me', said Pococurante. 'At one time I was made to believe that I took pleasure in reading it. But the continual repetition of battles, which are all alike—those gods, who are always busy achieving nothing—that Helen, who is the cause of the war, yet scarcely plays a part in the whole performance—that interminable and ineffectual siege—I have found them all insufferably tedious. I have several times asked well-read men if they were as much wearied by the work as I was. All the honest ones confessed that they fell asleep while reading it, but had to have it in their libraries, like some rusty old medal that has no commercial value.'

'But Your Excellency surely does not hold the same opinion of Virgil?' asked Candide.

'I grant that the second, fourth and sixth books of his *Æneid* are excellent. But his pious Æneas, strong Cloanthus, faithful Achates, little Ascanius, and that imbecile King

Latinus and that vulgar Amata—nothing could be more flat or disagreeable. I prefer Tasso, or even that sleepy tale-teller Ariosto.'

'May I take the liberty to ask, sir, if you do not take great pleasure from reading Horace?'

'There are maxims in this writer from which a man of the world may get some benefit; and the expressive energy of the verse fixes them more easily in the memory. But I care little for his journey to Brindisi, and his account of a bad dinner; or for his fishwives' quarrel between one Rupilius, whose words he describes as being "full of poisonous filth", and some other person, whose words were "dipped in vinegar". I was disgusted by his coarse lampoons against old women and witches; nor do I see the merit of his telling his friend Mæcenas that, if he will but rank him amongst lyric poets, his "lofty head shall touch the stars". Fools have a habit of believing that everything written by a famous author is admirable. For my part, I read only to please myself, and like only what suits my taste.'

Candide, who had been brought up never to form an opinion of his own, was astonished at all this. Martin, how-ever, thought Pococurante's attitude very reasonable.

'Ah, here's a Cicero', said Candide. 'This great man, I fancy, you are never tired of reading!'

'I never read him at all. What do I care for his pleadings for Rabirius or Cluentius? I try causes enough myself. I might have got along better with his philosophic works—except that, when I found he doubted of everything, I concluded that I knew as much as he, and had no need of a guide to ignorance.'

'Ah, but see these four-score volumes of Memoirs of the Academy of Sciences', said Martin. 'There may be some-thing good there.'

'There would be, if any of the compilers of this rubbish

had so much as invented the art of pin-making. But all these books are filled with empty abstractions, without one item of practical use.'

'What a prodigious number of plays!' said Candide, turning to another group of shelves: 'in Italian, in Spanish, in French!'

'Yes, there are three thousand of them, and not three good ones. And as for all these collections of sermons, which all put together are not worth a page of Seneca, and all these volumes of theology—you can well believe that neither I nor anyone else ever opens them.'

Martin noticed some shelves of English books. 'I fancy', he said to the senator, 'that a Republican like yourself must take pleasure in most of these works, imbued as they are with so liberal a spirit.'

'Yes, it is fine to write what one thinks: it is the privilege of a man. Throughout Italy, we write only what we do not think. The modern inhabitants of the land of the Cæsars and of Antoninus dare not have a single idea without permission from a Jacobin monk.

'I should be enamoured of the sense of liberty that inspires the geniuses of England, were it not that all that is good in this fair liberty of theirs is corrupted by petty passions and the spirit of party.'

Candide saw a collection of the works of Milton, and asked the senator if he did not think that author a great man. 'Who?' said Pococurante. 'That barbarian who writes a long commentary, in ten books of stumbling verse, on the first chapter of Genesis? That slovenly imitator of the Greeks, who has made grotesque nonsense of the story of the Creation? On the one hand, we have his Moses representing the Deity as making the world from the Word— yet his Messiah takes a large pair of compasses from the heavenly cupboard, to trace out his intended work!

'How could I have any esteem for a writer who has spoiled Tasso's *Hell and Devil*? Who transforms Lucifer sometimes into a toad, and sometimes into a pygmy? Who makes him repeat the same arguments a hundred times, and turns him into a theological casuist? A writer who borrows from Ariosto's comic invention of firearms, and absurdly turns it into a grave tale of the devils firing off canon in heaven?

'Neither I nor any other Italian can take any pleasure in all these dreary extravagances. The *Marriage of Sin and Death,* and all that account of Sin delivering snakes from her womb, are enough to make a man of any sensibility vomit. As for that long description of a hospital—it is fit reading only for a sexton.

'This obscure, bizarre and disgusting poem was slighted at its first publication. I only treat the author now as he was treated in his own country by his contemporaries.

'Such are my sentiments. I speak my mind, and am perfectly indifferent whether others think as I do.'

Candide was grieved, for he had a great respect for Homer, and was rather fond of Milton. 'Alas,' he whispered to Martin, 'I fear that this man must hold our German poets in great contempt.'

'There would be no great harm in that', said Martin.

'What a superior being!' Candide muttered between his teeth. 'What a great genius is this Pococurante! Nothing is good enough for him.'

They next went down to the garden, and Candide complimented the senator on its various adornments. 'It is all in very bad taste', said the owner. ''Tis a mere collection of gewgaws. But tomorrow I shall have another laid out upon a grander scale.'

When the two sightseers had taken leave of His Excellency, Candide remarked to Martin: 'Well, I think that now you will own that we have met the happiest of mortals—for he feels himself superior to everything that he possesses.'

'Do you not see', said Martin, 'that everything he possesses disgusts him? Plato has observed that the best stomachs are not those that reject all food.'

'But there must be some pleasure in condemning everything—in perceiving faults where others think they see beauties.'

'You mean, there is pleasure in having no pleasure.'

'Well, well, it seems that the only happy man will be I myself, when I see Cunégonde again.'

'It is always good to hope.'

But the days and weeks passed by, with no news of Cacambo. Candide was so overwhelmed with grief that he did not even notice the ingratitude of Paquette and Friar Giroflée, who never came to see him.

CHAPTER XXVI

SUPPER WITH SIX KINGS

CANDIDE, Martin and the other guests at the inn were just going to supper, when a man with a face the colour of soot came up behind Candide, took him by the arm, and said: 'Hold yourself ready to go along with us, without fail.'

It was Cacambo. Almost beside himself with joy, Candide embraced his dear friend. 'Cunégonde must be here too, I suppose?' he said. 'Where is she? Lead me to her, that I may die of joy in her presence!'

'Cunégonde is not here', said Cacambo. 'She is at Constantinople.'

'Good Heavens, Constantinople! But no matter—if she were in China, I would fly thither. Let us be gone!'

'We will go after supper. I can say no more to you now.

I am a slave, and my master waits for me. I must go and attend him at table. But say not a word, only get your supper and hold yourself ready.'

In a turmoil of emotions—delighted to have met his faithful agent again, astonished to hear that he was a slave, obsessed with the prospect of recovering his mistress—Candide sat down to supper. At table with him were Martin, who had listened unemotionally to his conversation with Cacambo, and six strangers who had come to Venice to take part in the carnival.

Cacambo, who was in attendance upon one of these strangers, said to him towards the end of the meal: 'Sire, Your Majesty can go when he pleases, the ship is ready.' After saying this, he left the room. The guests at the other tables looked at each other in surprise, but said nothing.

Another servant went up to his master, and said: 'Sire, Your Majesty's chaise is at Padua, and the bark is ready'. At a sign from the master, the servant withdrew.

The surprise of the company grew. A third servant went up to a third of the strangers, and said: 'Sire, believe me, Your Majesty had better not make any longer stay in this place. I will go and get everything ready.' This servant also immediately went out.

Candide and Martin took it for granted that these people were characters in a carnival masquerade. A fourth servant said to a fourth master: 'Your Majesty may set off when he pleases', and also went out. A fifth servant said the same to a fifth master. A sixth servant, however—whose master was sitting next to Candide—made a different remark. 'Troth, Sire,' he said, 'they will no longer trust Your Majesty, nor myself neither. We may both of us be sent to jail this very night. I go to make my own arrangements—and so, Sire, adieu.'

The six strangers, Candide and Martin sat in deep silence, until Candide broke it. 'Gentlemen,' he said, 'this is very droll. How came you all to be kings? I must confess that my friend Martin here and myself are but commoners.'

Cacambo's master answered gravely, in Italian: 'I am not joking. My name is Achmet III.[1] For many years I was Grand Sultan. I dethroned my brother, my nephew dethroned me; my viziers were beheaded, and I pass my declining years in the Old Seraglio. My nephew, the Grand Sultan Mahomet, gives me permission to travel sometimes for my health; and I am come to spend the carnival at Venice.'

A young man who sat next to Achmet spoke next: 'My name is Ivan.[2] I was once Czar of all the Russias, but was dethroned in my cradle. My father and mother were imprisoned, and I was brought up in jail. I am sometimes allowed to travel, accompanied by my warders; and I am come to spend the carnival at Venice.'

A third said: 'I am Charles Edward,[3] King of England. My father abdicated the throne in my favour. I have fought in defence of my rights, and eight hundred of my friends have had their hearts torn out of their bodies and thrown in their faces. I myself have been confined in a prison. I am going to Rome to visit the King my father, who was dethroned like myself and my grandfather; and I am come to spend the carnival at Venice.'

The fourth said: 'I am the King of Poland.[4] The fortune

[1] Succeeded his brother, Mustapha II, in 1703. Dethroned by the Janissaries in 1730, died in 1736.

[2] Born in 1730, dethroned in the same year, imprisoned, and finally stabbed to death in 1762.

[3] 'Bonnie Prince Charlie', the Young Pretender. He died in Florence in 1788.

[4] Augustus, Elector of Saxony and King of Poland, expelled from his kingdom in the war of 1756.

of war has stripped me of my dominions. My father suffered the same mishap. I resign myself to the will of Providence, like Sultan Achmet, Czar Ivan and King Charles Edward, whom God long preserve; and I am come to spend the carnival at Venice.'

The fifth said: 'I am King of Poland also.[1] I have twice lost my kingdom; but Providence has given me another domain, where I have done more good than all the Sarmatian kings put together were ever able to do on the banks of the Vistula. I resign myself likewise to Providence; and I am come to spend the carnival at Venice.'

The sixth monarch said: 'Gentlemen, I am not so great a prince as any of you. But I am, for all that, a king like any other. I am Theodore, elected King of Corsica.[2] I have had the title of Majesty, and now am scarcely granted the title of "Signor". I have minted my own money, and now do not possess a farthing. I have had two Secretaries of State, and now scarcely have a valet. I once sat on a throne, and since then have lain upon a truss of straw in a London jail. I very much fear that I shall meet the same fate here, although I am but come, like Your Majesties, to spend the carnival at Venice.'

This last utterance filled the other five kings with noble compassion. Each of them gave King Theodore twenty sequins with which to buy some suits of clothes and shirts. Candide gave him a diamond worth two thousand sequins.

---

[1] Stanislas Leszczynski, father-in-law of Louis XV, after losing the throne of Poland received the non-hereditary sovereignty of the Duchies of Bar and Lorraine, where he won the title 'The Beneficent'.

[2] Baron Theodor Neuhof, born in Metz in 1690, soldier of fortune who helped the Corsicans to rebel against the Genoese and was proclaimed their king, but left Corsica in fear of assassination eight months later. Died in London in 1756.

'Who is this man,' said one of the kings, 'who is able to give—and, what is more, has given—a hundred times as much as each of us? Are you also a king, sir?'

'No, sir,' said Candide, 'and I do not wish to be.'

As they were leaving the table, four Serene Highnesses came in. They also had lost their territories, and had come to spend the remainder of the carnival at Venice. But Candide paid no attention to these newcomers: all that he cared about was to go to Constantinople in search of Cunégonde.

CHAPTER XXVII

VOYAGE TO CONSTANTINOPLE

CACAMBO had hired cabins for Candide and Martin on the Turkish ship that was to carry Sultan Achmet back to Constantinople. After prostrating themselves before his unhappy Highness, they embarked.

'How strange to sup with six kings,' said Candide, as they were going on board, 'and one of them so poor that I gave him charity! Perhaps there may be many other princes still more unfortunate.

'For my part, I have lost only eighty sheep laden with treasure, and I am flying to the arms of Cunégonde. I say it once more, my dear Martin: Pangloss was in the right —everything is for the best.'

'I hope it may be.'

'But truly, was not that an improbable adventure? Never before has anyone seen or heard of six dethroned monarchs supping together at an inn.'

'It is not more extraordinary than most of the things that have happened to us. It is not unusual for kings to be dethroned; and as for our having had the honour to sup with six of them, it is a mere trifle, unworthy of note. What does it matter with whom one sups, so long as the fare is good?'

On board the vessel Candide fell on the neck of his old servant and friend Cacambo. 'What news of Cunégonde?' he said. 'Is she still a paragon of beauty? Does she still love me? How does she do? You have doubtless purchased a palace for her at Constantinople.'

'My dear master, Cunégonde washes dishes on the banks of the Propontis, in the house of a prince who has very few dishes to wash. She is a slave of a former sovereign named Rakoczy,[1] to whom the Grand Turk allows three crowns a day to maintain him in his exile. What is worse, she has lost her beauty and is grown very ugly.'

'Ugly or handsome, I am a man of honour, and am bound to love her always. But how can she have been reduced to such an abject condition, with the five or six millions that you brought her?'

'I will tell you. First, I was obliged to give two millions to Señor Don Fernando d'Ibarro y Figueora y Mascarenes y Lampourdos y Souza, Governor of Buenos Aires, for liberty to take Mistress Cunégonde away with me. Then a pirate stripped us of the rest. This same pirate carried us to Cape Matapan, to Milo, to Nicaria, to Samos, to Petra, to the Dardanelles and to Scutari. Cunégonde and the old woman are now in the house of the prince I told you of, and I myself am slave to the dethroned Sultan.'

'What a chain of dreadful disasters! But, after all, I still have some diamonds left. I can easily set Cunégonde free. . . It is a pity that she is grown ugly.

[1] Ferencz Rakoczy, a Transylvanian prince, stirred the Hungarians to revolt against the Hapsburgs, and fought successively against Leopold I and Joseph I. Finally defeated, he retired to Turkey and died at Rodosto in 1735.

'What think you?' Candide continued, speaking now to Martin. 'Who is most to be pitied, Sultan Achmet, Czar Ivan, King Charles Edward or I?'

'I cannot tell. To find the answer, I would have to enter into all your hearts.'

'Ah, if Pangloss were here, he would know the answer, and would tell us it.'

'I know not in what balance your Pangloss can weigh human misfortunes. I suppose, however, that there are millions of men on earth who are a hundred times more to be pitied than King Charles Edward, Czar Ivan or Sultan Achmet.'

'That may well be.'

A few days later they reached the entrance to the Black Sea. Candide paid a heavy ransom for Cacambo, and they and Martin transferred themselves to a galley that would take them to the shore of the Propontis. However ugly Cunégonde might have become, Candide was resolved to find her.

Amongst the crew of convicts on this galley were two who rowed very awkwardly, so that the Levantine captain kept lashing their bare backs with a bull's pizzle. Candide noticed them especially, as he felt sorry for them. Their disfigured features seemed rather like those of Pangloss and the unlucky Jesuit baron, Cunégonde's brother. The resemblance touched and saddened Candide, and he looked at the two men still more attentively. 'In troth,' he said to Cacambo, 'if I had not seen Master Pangloss hanged, and myself had the misfortune to kill the Baron, I should believe that they were among the rowers.'

On hearing the words 'Pangloss' and 'the Baron', the two convicts uttered a cry and stopped rowing, letting go of the oars. The Levantine captain rushed up to them and applied his bull's pizzle harder than ever. 'Hold, hold, signor,' Candide shouted, 'I will give you all the money you ask!'

'Why, it is Candide!' the two convicts exclaimed.

'Do I dream?' said Candide. 'Am I awake? Am I actually on board this galley? Is this my Lord Baron, whom I killed? And Master Pangloss, whom I saw hanged?'

'Yes, 'tis we, 'tis we!'

'What, is this the great philosopher?' said Martin.

'Hark ye, captain,' said Candide, 'what ransom do you ask for the Baron von Thunder-ten-Tronckh, one of the first barons of the Reich, and for Dr. Pangloss, the most profound metaphysician in Germany?'

'Dog of a Christian,' said the Levantine, 'since these two dogs of Christian convicts are barons and metaphysicians—which doubtless are high titles in their country—why, then, thou shalt give me fifty thousand sequins.'

'You shall have them, sir. Carry me back with the speed of lightning to Constantinople, and you shall be paid immediately. No! Rather carry me first to Mistress Cunégonde.'

But the captain had already, on hearing the first order, started turning the ship round on a course for Constantinople. He made the crew row so hard that the vessel seemed to fly like a bird.

Candide embraced the Baron and Pangloss again and again. 'And how is it, my dear Baron, that I did not kill you? And you, my dear Pangloss, how are you come to life again after your hanging? And why are you both on this Turkish galley?'

'Is it true that my dear sister is in this country?' 'Is it really my dear Candide?' asked the Baron and Pangloss.

'Yes, it is', said Candide to both questions. He introduced Martin and Cacambo to the two others, and there were embraces and voluble conversation all round.

The galley quickly brought them to port, and a Jewish merchant was fetched, to whom Candide sold for fifty thousand sequins a diamond worth double that amount—although the Jew swore by Abraham that he could not give more. Pangloss and the Baron were set free: the former flung himself weeping at the feet of his benefactor, whilst the latter nodded his thanks, and promised to return the money at the first opportunity.

'But is it possible', the Baron asked, 'that my sister should be in Turkey?'

'It is more than possible; it is certain', said Candide. 'She scours the dishes in the house of a Transylvanian prince.'

Two more Jews were fetched, Candide sold more diamonds, and they all set out, in another galley, to liberate Cunégonde.

CHAPTER XXVIII

THE GALLEY-SLAVES' STORIES

'ONCE again, I ask your pardon, Reverend Father,' said Candide, 'for running you through the body.'

'Let us say no more about it. I must own that I myself was a little hasty. But since you wish to know by what accident I came to be on board that galley, I will tell you.

'The College apothecary cured me of the wound you gave me. Some time afterwards I was attacked and taken prisoner by a party of Spanish troops, who clapped me in prison at Buenos Aires, just after my sister had left that city.

'I asked leave to return to Rome, to see the General of my order. He appointed me chaplain to the French ambassador at Constantinople.

'I had not been a week in my new office, when I met one evening a very handsome young *icoglan*. The weather was hot, and the young man had an inclination to bathe. I took the opportunity to bathe likewise. I did not know that it was a capital crime for a Christian to be found naked with a young Mussulman. A cadi ordered me to receive a hundred blows on the soles of my feet, and sent me to the galleys—a most horrible injustice!

'But now I would fain know, how came my sister to be here in Turkey as scullion to a Transylvanian prince?'

'But you, my dear Pangloss,' said Candide, 'how comes it that I see you again?'

'You saw me hanged, as you thought', said Pangloss. 'I ought properly to have been burnt; but, as you will remember, it rained in torrents just as they were about to roast me. They could not even light the fire: so they hanged me, because they could do no better.

'A surgeon bought my body, carried me home and dissected me. He began by making a crucial incision from my navel to the clavicle.

'I had been shockingly badly hanged. The High Executioner of the Holy Inquisition, who was a subdeacon, was an excellent hand at burning people; but as for hanging, he was not used to it. The cord was wet and did not slip properly, and the noose was not tight. In short, I continued to breathe. The crucial incision made me roar out so loud that the surgeon fell over backwards. He imagined that he had been dissecting the devil, ran away in terror and tumbled down the staircase. The noise brought his wife from an adjoining room. She saw me stretched upon the table with my crucial incision, became still more terrified than her husband, and ran away and fell over him.

'After all this confusion, I heard the wife say to her husband: "My love, how could you think of dissecting a heretic? Don't you know that they have the devil in their bodies? I'll run directly for a priest to come and exorcise him."

'I was horrified at this proposal, and gathered what little strength I had left to cry out: "Mercy! Mercy!" At length the Portuguese barber took courage, and sewed up my wound. His wife nursed me, and in a fortnight I was upon my legs.

'The barber got me a place as lacquey to a Knight of Malta, who was going to Venice. But this man had no money to pay my wages, so I entered the service of a Venetian merchant, and went with him to Constantinople.

'One day I took a notion to enter a mosque. Nobody was there but an old imam and a very pretty young female, who was saying her prayers. Her throat was bare, and in her bosom she had a beautiful nosegay of tulips, roses, anemones, ranunculuses, hyacinths and auriculas. She let her nosegay fall: I picked it up, and most respectfully returned it to her. But I was so long in putting it in place, that the imam grew angry. Seeing that I was a Christian, he cried out for help. They carried me before a cadi, who ordered me to receive a hundred blows on the soles of my feet, and sent me to the galleys.

'I was chained in the very same galley, and to the very same bench, as his lordship. The rest of the crew consisted of four young men from Marseilles, five Neapolitan priests, and two monks from Corfu. I learnt from my fellow-slaves that adventures similar to mine were very common.

'His lordship always claimed that he had suffered a worse injustice than I; but I used to insist that it was much more permissible to replace a nosegay in a young woman's bosom than to be found naked with a young *icoglan*. We were continually disputing this point, and in consequence were frequently lashed with a bull's pizzle. But at last the concatenation of sublunary events brought you on board our galley to ransom us.'

'Tell me, my dear Pangloss, when you had been hanged,

dissected, and whipped, and were tugging at an oar in a galley, did you continue to think that everything was for the best?'

'I retain my first opinion. After all, I am a philosopher, and it would not become me to contradict myself. Besides, Leibnitz cannot be wrong, and the doctrine of the pre-established harmony is the finest thing in the world—as also are the *plenum* and the *materia subtilis*.'

CHAPTER XXIX

CUNÉGONDE FOUND AGAIN

As the party approached the house of the Transylvanian prince, they saw Cunégonde and the old woman hanging cloths on a line.

The Baron turned pale at the sight, and even Candide, that faithful lover, was horrified. The lovely Cunégonde was burnt black by the sun, her eyes were bloodshot, her neck withered, her cheeks wrinkled and her arms covered with a red scurf. Candide recoiled for an instant, but good manners made him go forward. Cunégonde and the old woman embraced Candide and the Baron. Candide then ransomed the two women.

There was a small farm in the neighbourhood, and the old woman suggested that Candide should rent this as a temporary lodging for the whole party. Cunégonde did not know that she had grown ugly, as nobody had told her. She reminded Candide of his promises in so peremptory a manner that the good-natured youth did not dare to refuse her. He told the Baron that he was going to marry his sister.

'I will never suffer such baseness on my sister's part,' said the Baron, 'or such insolence on yours. I will never be reproached with such a disgrace. Why, my sister's children would not be received in the chapter-houses of Germany! No, my sister shall never marry any person below the rank of a baron of the Reich.'

Cunégonde fell weeping at her brother's feet, but he was inflexible. 'Silly fellow,' said Candide, 'have I not delivered thee from the galleys, paid thy ransom and thy sister's, too, who was a dish-washer and is very ugly? I have the goodness to make her my wife, and thou still dost set thyself up to oppose the match! If I were to give rein to my anger, I should kill thee again.'

'Thou mayst kill me again,' said the Baron, 'but thou shalt not marry my sister while I am living.'

CHAPTER XXX

PHILOSOPHY ON THE PROPONTIS

AT the bottom of his heart Candide had no wish to marry Cunégonde. But the Baron's insolence made him determined to do so, and Cunégonde pressed him so warmly that he could not recant.

He consulted Pangloss, Martin and Cacambo. Pangloss drew up a fine memorial proving that the Baron had no rights over his sister, and that by the laws of the Reich she could marry Candide morganatically. Martin advised throwing the Baron into the sea. Cacambo suggested that he should be handed over to the Levantine skipper and put back to work in the galleys: after which he could be sent by the first ship to the Father General in Rome.

This suggestion found general favour. The old woman was told of it, and approved, but nothing was said about it to Cunégonde. The transaction was carried out, for a little money: and they had the double pleasure of tricking a Jesuit and punishing the pride of a German baron.

The reader might well suppose that Candide—having, after so many misadventures, got married to his mistress; being blessed with the company of the philosophers Pangloss and Martin, the shrewd Cacambo and the old woman; and having, moreover, brought back so many diamonds from the land of the ancient Incas—would now live happily ever afterwards.

What in fact happened was this: Candide was so badly cheated by the Jews that in the end he had nothing but his little farm. His wife, who grew uglier every day, became sour-tempered and insupportable. The old woman was ailing, and became even worse-humoured than Cunégonde. Cacambo, who worked in the garden and carried its produce to market in Constantinople, became worn out with toil and felt utterly miserable. Pangloss was gloomy at not being a shining light in some German university. As for Martin, he was convinced that one is equally badly off wherever one is, so he bore everything with patience.

Candide, Martin and Pangloss sometimes had discussions on metaphysics and ethics. Boats passed under the windows of the farm, carrying effendis, pashas and cadis off to exile in Lemnos, Mitylene or Erzerum. Other cadis, pashas and effendis could be seen coming to replace the exiles, and later being exiled in their turn. The boats also carried heads, neatly fixed on poles, which were being sent as gifts to the Sublime Porte. Such sights increased the philosophers' zeal for argument.

When they were not arguing, time hung so heavily on their hands that one day the old woman remarked: 'I wonder which is worse: to be ravished a hundred times by negro pirates, to have one buttock cut off, to run the gauntlet among the Bulgarians, to be dissected and to be a galley-slave; or to stay here doing nothing?'

'That', said Candide, 'is a very profound question.' It started them off on further discussions. Martin had come to the conclusion that it is man's fate to live either in agonies of fear and turmoil or in the prostration of boredom. Candide did not entirely agree, but could not make up his mind. Pangloss, whilst admitting that he had undergone dreadful sufferings, still maintained that everything was marvellously good—although he did not believe it.

Something happened that confirmed Martin in his detestable beliefs, made Candide hesitate more than ever, and even caused embarrassment to Pangloss. This was the arrival of Paquette and Friar Giroflée. They were penniless, having quickly run through the three thousand piastres that Candide had given them. They had parted, been reconciled and had quarrelled again. They had been imprisoned, and had escaped. Friar Giroflée had turned Turk as he once said he might. Paquette continued to ply her trade wherever she went, but earned little by it.

'I told you', Martin said to Candide, 'that your gift would soon be squandered, and would only make them more miserable. You and Cacambo have poured out millions of piastres, yet you are no happier than Friar Giroflée and Paquette.'

Pangloss had a few observations to make to Paquette. 'So, my poor child,' he said, 'Heaven has brought you here among us again. Do you know that you have cost me the tip of my nose, one eye and one ear? Ah me, to what have you been reduced—and what a world is this of ours!'

This new event made them all philosophize more than ever.

There lived in the neighbourhood a very famous dervish, who was generally considered the best philosopher in Turkey. One day they went to consult him. Pangloss, as their spokesman, said to the dervish: 'Master, we come to entreat you to tell us, why so strange an animal as man was created?'

'Why do you meddle with the matter?' said the dervish. 'Is it any business of yours?'

'But, Reverend Father,' said Candide, 'there is a horrible deal of evil on earth.'

'What signifies it whether there is evil or good? When the Sultan sends a ship to Egypt, does he trouble his head whether the rats in the hold are at ease or not?'

'What, then, should one do?'

'One should be silent.'

'I offered myself the flattering prospect', said Candide, 'of debating with you a little concerning causes and effects, the best of possible worlds, the origin of evil, the nature of the soul, the pre-established harmony, and similar matters.'

At these words the dervish shut the door in their faces.

That same day news had come from Constantinople that two Viziers of the Bench and the Grand Mufti had been strangled, and that several of their friends had been impaled. This catastrophe caused a considerable stir for a few hours. On their way back from the dervish's house, the philosophers met a worthy old man taking the air at his door, under an arbour of orange-trees. Pangloss, who besides being a philosopher was also keenly interested in gossip, asked him if he knew the name of the strangled Mufti.

'No,' said the old man, 'I have never in my life known the name of any Mufti or Vizier; nor do I know anything of the event you speak of. I take the view that, in general, those who meddle in politics tend to come to miserable ends, and deserve to do so. But I never inquire what is doing at Constantinople. I am contented with sending thither for sale the fruits of my garden.'

He invited the foreigners into his house, where his two daughters and two sons brought them home-made sherbets of various kinds, of caymac flavoured with the peels of candied citrons, oranges, lemons, pineapples, dates, pistachio nuts and Mocha coffee—which last was unadulterated with the inferior coffee of Batavia or the American islands. After this the two daughters perfumed the guests' beards.

'You must have a very large estate', Candide said to the old man.

'I have no more than twenty acres, which I dig with the help of my children. Labour holds off three great evils: tedium, vice and poverty.'

On their way home, Candide thought over the old Turk's words. 'This old worthy', said he, 'seems to have created for himself a destiny highly preferable to those of the six kings with whom we supped.'

'Elevated stations', said Pangloss, 'are often very dangerous: so all the philosophers testify. Eglon, King of Moab, was assassinated by Aod. Absalom was hanged by his hair and run through with three darts. King Nadab, son of Jeroboam, was killed by Baaza; King Ela by Zimri; Okosias by Jehu; Athaliah by Jehoiada. The Kings Jehoiakim, Jeconiah and Zedekiah were led into captivity. You know what befel Crœsus, Astyages, Darius, Dionysus of Syracuse, Pyrrhus, Perseus, Hannibal, Jugurtha, Ariovistus, Cæsar, Pompey, Nero, Otho, Vitellius, Domitian, Richard II of England, Edward II, Henry VI, Richard III, Mary Stuart, Charles I, the three Henries of France and the Emperor Henry IV. You know also—'

'I know also', said Candide, 'that we must dig in our garden.'

'You are in the right,' said Pangloss, 'for when man was put into the garden of Eden he was put there *ut operaretur eum*—that he might till it, that he might work: which proves that man was not born to be idle.'

'Let us work, then, and not argue', said Martin. 'It is the only way to render life supportable.'

All the members of the little society entered into this laudable design, and set themselves to exercise their various talents. Their small farm yielded good crops. Cunégonde continued to be very ugly, but she became an excellent pastrycook. Paquette embroidered. The old woman laundered. Even Friar Giroflée turned out useful: he proved to be a very good carpenter, and even quite a decent fellow.

Pangloss would often say to Candide: 'There is certainly a concatenation of events in this best of all possible worlds. Consider: had you not been kicked out of a fine castle for love of Mistress Cunégonde—had you not come under the Inquisition—had you not travelled over America on foot—had you not run the Baron through the body—had you not lost your sheep from the good country of El Dorado—why, then, you would not now be here, to eat candied citrons and pistachio nuts.'

'That is excellently observed', said Candide. 'But let us dig in our garden.'

CANDIDE

PART II

CANDIDE, OR OPTIMISM

PART II

CHAPTER I

CANDIDE SETS OUT AGAIN

IN the end everything in life grows wearisome. Riches exhaust their possessor; ambition, once satisfied, leaves behind only regrets; the sweets of love are not sweet for long.

Candide, that man so versed in fortune's ups and downs, soon became tired of digging in his garden. 'We may be living in the best of all possible worlds, Master Pangloss,' he said, 'but you will confess, at least, that I for my part am not enjoying my share of all possible happiness. Here I live on an obscure corner of the Propontis, with no other means of livelihood than my own labour, which may one day fail me; no other pleasures than those I get from Cunégonde, who is very ugly and, which is worse, my wife; no other companions than yourself, whom I sometimes find tedious —Martin, who gives me the spleen—Giroflée, who is but very lately become an honest man—Paquette, the risks of whose companionship you know—and the old woman, who has only one buttock, and whose stories send a man to sleep on his feet.'

'Philosophy teaches us', said Pangloss, 'that monads, divisible *ad infinitum*, arrange themselves with wonderful sagacity to form the various bodies that we observe in nature. The heavenly bodies are what they ought to be; they are placed where they ought to be placed; they describe the circles they ought to describe. Man follows the bent he ought to follow; he is what he ought to be; he does what he ought to do.

'You, Candide, complain because the monad of your soul is bored. But the state of being bored is but a modification of the soul: and this does not alter the truth that everything is for the best, both for you and for others.

'When you saw me covered with sores, this did not alter my opinion; for if Paquette had not caused me to taste the pleasures and poison of love, I should not have met with you in Holland; I should not have afforded James the Anabaptist the opportunity of performing a meritorious action; I should not have been hanged in Lisbon, for my neighbour's edification; and I should not now be here, to fortify you with my advice, so that you may live and die a disciple of Leibnitz.

'Yes, my dear Candide, everything is linked together, everything is necessary in this best of all possible worlds. It is necessary that the burgher of Montauban should be the preceptor of princes; that the worm of Quimper-Corentin should carp, carp, carp; that the informer against the philosophers should have had himself crucified in the Rue St. Denis; that a little sizar of the Recollets and the Archdeacon of St. Malo should distil gall and calumny from their Christian Journals; that philosophy should be impeached in the court of Melpomene—and that philosophers should continue to enlighten mankind, despite the croakings of the ridiculous brutes that flounder in the swamps of literature.

'As for you, even should you once more be expelled with kicks from the finest of castles; once more be taught drill and tactics, and the art of running the gauntlet, amongst the Bulgarians; once more be soused by a Dutchwoman's zealotry—flogged by the Most Holy Inquisition— endangered amongst the Oreillons and the French; in short, were you to suffer anew all possible calamities, you would still maintain that everything is for the best, that the *plenum*, the *materia subtilis*, the pre-established harmony and the monads are the finest things in creation, and that Leibnitz is a great man, even for those who do not understand him.'

Candide, despite the fact that he had killed three men, including two priests, was the mildest of creatures, and said nothing to all this. But he was tired of the doctor, and of all his company. At dawn the following day he took a white staff and set off, in no particular direction, looking for a place where he would not be bored, and where human beings would be as they are in the good land of El Dorado—that is to say, something other than human.

Feeling all the better for no longer being in love with Cunégonde, he journeyed on—living on the bounty of various peoples who, strange as it may sound, do, in fact, give alms, although they are not Christian—until, after a long and arduous tramp, he arrived at Tauris, on the Persian frontier, a city noted for the atrocities committed there by Turks and Persians in turn.

By this time Candide was utterly exhausted, and had scarcely enough clothing left for the barest modesty. He was becoming less and less a believer in the doctrines of Pangloss when one day he met a Persian who very politely begged him to ennoble his house with his presence.

'You are laughing at me', said Candide. 'I am a poor devil, who has left a wretched cottage on the Propontis because I was married to Mistress Cunégonde, who is grown very ugly, and because I was bored almost to death. I am not, indeed, made to ennoble anybody's house. I am not even noble myself: for which God be thanked, since, had I been so, the Herr Baron von Thunder-ten-Tronckh would have paid very dearly for the kicks that he was so gracious as to bestow upon me; or else I should have had to die of shame—not but what that would have been pretty philosophical. Besides, I have been ignominiously whipped by the executioners of the Most Holy Inquisition, as well as by two thousand heroes at three-halfpence a day. Give me alms, if you please, but do not insult my poverty with railleries which would take away all the merit of your beneficence.'

'My Lord,' replied the Persian, 'you may be a mendicant —and indeed it seems plain enough that you are one. But my religion obliges me to hospitality. It is enough that you are a man, and in distress, that the apple of my eye should be the path for your feet. Vouchsafe, then, to ennoble my house with your radiant presence.'

'I will do whatever you wish.'

'Come, then, enter.'

During the next few days Candide was amazed at the courtesy and consideration shown him by his host. The slaves anticipated his wishes, and the whole function of the household seemed to be to serve his pleasure. 'If this does but last,' thought Candide, 'everything is not too bad in this country.' By the third day he was again convinced that Pangloss was a great philosopher.

CHAPTER II

THE HOSPITABLE PERSIAN

WELL fed, well clad and free from all worry, Candide soon became as ruddy-cheeked, fresh and handsome as he had been in Westphalia.

His host, Ismael Raab, was delighted at the change in him. Raab himself was a man six feet tall, with small, deeply bloodshot eyes and a large, pimply nose that proclaimed his disregard of the law of Mahomet. His whiskers were famous throughout the country: mothers prayed that their sons might have such a pair.

Raab had wives, for he was rich: but his disposition was of a sort that is sadly common in the East, as well as in some European colleges. 'Your Excellency is more beautiful than the stars', he one day said softly to Candide, stroking him under the chin. 'You must have captivated many hearts. You are made to give and to receive happiness.'

'Alas, I have had but one moment of half happiness, and that was behind a screen, where I was but awkwardly situated. Mistress Cunégonde was handsome in those days. . . .'

'Mistress Cunégonde! Poor innocent! Follow me, my Lord.' Candide did so. They arrived at a charming summer-house in the depths of a small wood—a spot dedicated, so it seemed, to silence and pleasure. Here Ismael Raab amorously embraced Candide and in a few words declared a passion similar to that so energetically expressed by the beautiful Alexis in one of Virgil's Eclogues.

Candide was astounded. 'No,' he exclaimed, 'I shall never suffer such infamy! What a cause, and what a horrible effect! I had rather die!'

'Die you shall, then,' said Ismael, enraged. 'How, thou Christian dog, because I politely wished to give thee pleasure . . . resolve directly to satisfy me, or to suffer the cruellest of deaths.'

Candide did not hesitate for long. He was appalled by the Persian's 'sufficing reason', but, on the other hand, he had a philosopher's fear of death.

We can become accustomed to anything. Well fed, well looked after, but always closely watched, Candide was not utterly disgusted with his condition. Good cheer, and the various amusements offered by Ismael's slaves, gave him respite from his sorrows. He was unhappy only when he thought: and that is true of the majority of mankind.

About this time the Reverend Ed-Ivan-Baal-Denk returned to Persia from Constantinople. This eminent divine was one of the mainstays of the church militant of Persia, and was also one of the most learned men of the Moslem world, with a fluent knowledge of Arabic and even of Greek —or of what nowadays passes for Greek in the country of Demosthenes and Sophocles. He had visited Constantinople in order to debate with the Reverend Mahmoud-Abram a very knotty point of doctrine—namely, whether the quill used by the Prophet to write the Koran had been plucked by him from the wing of the Archangel Gabriel, or whether Gabriel had freely made the Prophet a gift of it.

They had debated this point for seventy-two hours, with a heat worthy of the great days of philosophical argument. Ed-Ivan-Baal-Denk returned home convinced, like all the other disciples of Ali, that Mahomet plucked the quill. Mahmoud, like all the other sectaries of Omar, remained convinced that the Prophet could not have done anything so uncivil, and that Gabriel's gift of the quill was voluntary.

According to some reports, a bold, radical fellow in Constantinople suggested that it would be better first to find out whether the Koran had, in fact, been written with one of Gabriel's quills. He was stoned.

Candide's arrival in Tauris had been talked of widely. Several people who had heard him speak of 'contingent' and 'non-contingent' effects began to suspect that he was a philosopher. News of this reached Ed-Ivan-Baal-Denk, who expressed a wish to meet him. Raab could hardly refuse a person of such consequence, and Candide was led before the great man.

Ed-Ivan-Baal-Denk was highly satisfied with the way in which Candide discoursed on physical evil and moral evil, the agent and the actuated, and so forth. 'I see that you are a philosopher,' he said, 'and that is sufficient. It is not right that so great a man as yourself should be treated with the indignity of which I have heard tales. You are a foreigner, and Ismael Raab has no rights over you. I propose to introduce you at court. You will be well received: the Sophi has a passion for the sciences.

'Ismael, you will release this young philosopher into my hands, or dread incurring the displeasure of the Prince—not to speak of bringing down upon yourself the vengeance of Heaven, and especially of the monks.'

The amorous Persian was terrified into acquiescence. Candide gave thanks to Heaven and to the monks, and the same day set out with Ed-Ivan-Baal-Denk for Ispahan, where the population received them with enthusiasm.

CHAPTER III

A FAVOURITE OF THE SOPHI

ED-IVAN-BAAL-DENK presented Candide to the King without delay. His Majesty was delighted, and arranged debates between Candide and several of the Court scholars, who treated Candide as an ignorant fool: this greatly helped to convince His Majesty that Candide was a great man.

'You do not understand Candide's arguments,' said the King, 'so you talk nonsense to him. But I, who understand them no more than you do, can assure you that he is a great philosopher. I swear it by My Whiskers.' This utterance silenced the scholars.

Candide was lodged in the palace, and had slaves and magnificent clothes. The Sophi commanded that, whatever he might say, nobody should dare to contradict him. His

Majesty went even further: being repeatedly urged by Ed-Ivan-Baal-Denk to give Candide advancement, he one day decided to promote him to the rank of his most intimate favourites.

'God and the Prophet be praised,' Ed-Ivan-Baal-Denk said to Candide, 'I have most agreeable news for you. How fortunate you are, my dear Candide, how you will be envied! You shall swim in opulence, you may aspire to the highest posts in the Empire. Remember, my dear friend, that it was I who procured for you the favour that you are now to enjoy. The King grants you a token of his esteem that many have hotly sought: you will present a spectacle such as the Court has not enjoyed these two years past.'

'But what are these benefits that the Prince is so gracious as to bestow upon me?'

'This very day you will receive fifty strokes with a bull's pizzle on the soles of your feet, in His Majesty's presence. The eunuchs appointed to perfume you for the occasion will be here directly. Prepare yourself to pass cheerfully through this little trial, and thereby render yourself worthy of the King of Kings.'

'Let the King of Kings keep his favours to himself', Candide angrily exclaimed, 'if one must receive fifty strokes with a bull's pizzle to earn them.'

'It is the royal custom', Ed-Ivan-Baal-Denk said coldly, 'with those on whom His Majesty means to lavish his benefits. I love you too dearly to pay any heed to your little display of spleen, and I will make your fortune in spite of yourself.'

The eunuchs arrived, preceded by the Executor of His Majesty's Private Pleasures, who was one of the tallest and strongest lords of the court. Despite his protests and struggles, Candide's legs were perfumed, according to custom, and four eunuchs carried him between two files of soldiers to the place appointed for the ceremony. Meanwhile music played, cannon were fired, and the bells were rung in all the mosques of Ispahan.

The Sophi was already there, attended by his chief officers and the most eminent members of his court. Candide was stretched out on a small gilt bench, and the Executor of the Private Pleasures set to work.

'Master Pangloss, Master Pangloss, were you but here!' Candide shouted, blubbering and bawling with all his might. This would have been thought highly improper had not Ed-Ivan-Baal-Denk explained that his protégé acted thus only to give His Majesty the greater entertainment. The monarch was, in fact, laughing like a maniac, and was so pleased that when the fifty strokes had been given he ordered fifty more. But the Prime Minister, with unusual boldness, represented to His Majesty that such an unheard-of favour conferred on a foreigner might cause disaffection among his subjects. The King therefore countermanded his order, and Candide was carried to his apartment.

His feet were bathed in vinegar and he was put to bed. All the grandees came one after another to congratulate him. Then the Sophi himself came and, besides giving Candide his hand to kiss in the customary manner, actually deigned to strike him violently on the mouth. The politicians deduced from this that Candide would have a career almost without precedent—and in this, unusually for politicians, they were not mistaken.

CHAPTER IV

CANDIDE LOSES A LEG

WHEN Candide's wounds were healed he was led before His Majesty to thank him. The monarch received him with the most signal marks of favour: besides boxing his ears two or three times during the conversation, he afterwards conducted him back as far as the guardroom, repeatedly kicking his backside. The courtiers almost collapsed with envy: ever since His Majesty had instituted his custom of knocking about his favourites, no one had ever before had the honour of being knocked about as much as Candide.

Three days later Candide—who had been driven almost out of his mind by all these marks of favour, and had decided that, after all, everything was very bad—was appointed plenipotentiary Governor of Chusistan, with the right to wear a fur cap, which is a badge of great distinction in Persia. After taking leave of the Sophi, who honoured him with a few final endearments, he set out for Sus, the capital of his province.

Ever since Candide's first appearance at court the Imperial grandees had conspired against him. The uncommon favours that the Sophi had heaped on him had only intensified the storm that was shortly to burst over him. Candide meanwhile thought himself very fortunate, especially in being sent so far away. As he said to himself, with deep conviction:

Happy the subjects distant from their prince.

When they were still less than twenty miles from Ispahan, Candide and his party encountered five hundred heavily armed horsemen, who greeted them with a heavy fusillade. Candide at first thought that this was in his honour, but was disillusioned by a bullet that broke one of his legs. His men laid down their arms, and Candide, semi-conscious, was carried to a remote castle. His baggage, camels, slaves and white and black eunuchs, as well as thirty-six women whom the Sophi had given him for his private use, became spoils of the victor. Candide's leg was cut off, as a precaution against gangrene, and he was carefully kept alive, in readiness for a more cruel death.

'Ah, Pangloss, Pangloss!' Candide moaned, as soon as he could speak, 'what would become of your optimism if you could see me now, lacking a leg and in the hands of my bitterest enemies? And all just as I was entering upon the path of happiness, being Governor—or King, as one might say—of one of the greatest provinces of the ancient Median Empire, with camels, slaves, eunuchs black and white, as well as thirty-six women who were for my use and whom I had not used. . . .'

Meanwhile, however, the situation was developing in his favour. The Prime Minister had learnt of the outrage against him, and had sent a body of experienced troops in pursuit of the insurgents. Ed-Ivan-Baal-Denk had spread by means of his fellow-monks a report that Candide, being a work of the monks, was therefore a work of God. The clergy also published a guarantee, in the name of the Prophet, that anyone who had eaten pork, drunk wine, gone several days without bathing or had intercourse with women at an improper time, contrary to the prohibitions of the Koran, should *ipso facto* be absolved upon telling anything he knew of the conspiracy. The result was that the castle where Candide was held captive was soon discovered and stormed. Since the whole affair had now become one of religion, the vanquished were, of course, exterminated.

Freed from the worst danger he had ever yet undergone,

Candide clambered out of his jail over a pile of dead, and he and his attendants resumed the journey to his Governorship, where he was received with the deference due to a favourite who had been honoured with fifty strokes of a bull's pizzle on the soles of his feet in the presence of the King of Kings.

CHAPTER V

GOVERNOR CANDIDE

THE virtue of philosophy is in making us love our fellow creatures. Pascal is almost the only philosopher who seems to wish to make us hate them. Candide, luckily for him, had never read Pascal, and loved poor humanity with all his heart.

All persons of good will in Candide's province soon realized this. Previously they had always kept aloof from the *Missi Dominici* of the Empire; but now they were quite willing to assemble before Candide and give him their advice. He made many wise laws for the encouragement of agriculture, population, commerce and the arts. He rewarded those who had made useful experiments, and even encouraged those who had made nothing but books. 'When all the people in my province are contented,' he used to remark, 'perhaps I shall be, too.'

Candide knew little of human nature. He became the target of venomous lampoons, and was libellously attacked in a book entitled *The Friend of Mankind*. He found that by endeavouring to make men happy he had only made them ungrateful. 'What a plague it is,' he exclaimed, 'to rule over these unfledged creatures that infest the earth! Would I were still on the Propontis, with Master Pangloss, Cacambo, Mistress Cunégonde, the one-buttocked daughter of Pope Urban X, Friar Giroflée and the wanton Paquette.'

CHAPTER VI

CANDIDE'S SERAGLIO

In his bitterness Candide wrote a moving letter to Ed-Ivan-Baal-Denk, depicting his state of mind so vividly that the monk felt sorry for him, and persuaded the Sophi to relieve him of his post. In reward for his services His Majesty granted Candide a considerable pension.

Freed from the burden of greatness, Candide decided to seek the optimism of Pangloss in the pleasures of private life. Hitherto, in his devotion to the service of others, he had forgotten that he had a seraglio. He now remembered it—with the thrill that the mere name provokes. 'Let all be made ready', he said to his chief eunuch, 'for my visiting the women.'

'My Lord,' said the soprano gentleman, ''tis now that Your Excellency truly deserves the title of "the Wise". Men, for whom you have done so much, were not worthy of your care. But women, now. . .'

'That may be', Candide said modestly.

Deep in a garden, where art helped nature to unfold her beauties, stood a small house of simple and elegant design. This alone was enough to distinguish it from the buildings to be seen in the faubourgs of Europe's Most Beautiful City. As he approached the house, Candide could not help blushing. The air around breathed a delicious perfume. The flowers, amorously interlaced, seemed guided by the instinct of pleasure. Their beauty, moreover, was slow in fading: the blazing hue of the rose seemed never to grow dim. The view of a rock from which waters cascaded with a murmuring babble invited the soul to that soft melancholy which is the forerunner of sensual pleasure.

Quivering, Candide entered a large room furnished with taste and magnificence. His senses captivated by some secret spell, he gazed upon the young Telemachus—on canvas only, yet seeming to breathe—amidst the nymphs of Calypso's court; or at a naked Diana flying to the arms of passionate Endymion; or, with still greater agitation, at a Venus faithfully copied from her of Italy.

Suddenly he heard a divine harmony. A troop of young Georgian girls, wearing their veils, entered and danced around him in a ballet. The performance was charmingly designed and far more appropriate to the occasion than those trivial displays that one sees on mean stages after, say, some scene depicting the death of Cæsar or Pompey.

At a given signal all the veils were let fall, and the entertainment was further enlivened by the sight of vivid and animated countenances. The young beauties threw themselves into attitudes of studied seductiveness, which yet did not appear studied. One expressed in her glance an unbridled passion; another the soft languor that waits for pleasures without seeking them. A third bent forward and then quickly raised herself, to give a glimpse of those ravishing allurements that ladies display so freely in Paris. A fourth half opened her cymar, to reveal a leg that could inflame any man of feeling.

The dance stopped, and all the young beauties came to rest. The pause aroused Candide from stupor. Filled with raging desire, he gazed avidly around him—imprinted kisses on burning lips and swimming eyes—passed his hands over globes whiter than alabaster, whose heaving motion struggled against the touch—perceived little scarlet protuberances, like rosebuds waiting for the sun to open them, and kissed them rapturously, lingering as if his lips were glued to the spot.

Next, Candide gave himself up to the rapturous contemplation of female figures—some majestic, some slender and delicate. Finally, hot with passion, he threw his handkerchief to a young person whose gaze he had observed constantly fixed upon him. 'Teach me the meaning', she seemed to say, 'of a disquiet that I do not understand,' and to blush at the unspoken words, thus becoming a thousand times more lovely.

The eunuch opened the door of a chamber consecrated to the mysteries of love, and the lovers entered. ''Tis here that you will find happiness', the eunuch said to Candide.

'Indeed I hope so', Candide answered.

The ceilings and walls of the little room were covered with mirrors. In the middle of the floor was a couch of black satin. Candide threw the young Georgian on this, and with incredible speed undressed her. The sweet creature let him do as he pleased, interrupting him only with ardent kisses. 'My Lord,' she said, in typical Turkish style, 'how fortunate is your slave, how honoured by your transports!'

Passion can be expressed in any language, by those who truly feel it. These few words threw Candide into an ecstasy. He felt himself an entirely different person, and everything that he saw seemed utterly new. What a difference between Mistress Cunégonde, grown ugly and ravished by the Bulgarians, and a Georgian girl of eighteen who had never been ravished at all! Candide's enjoyment of her was the first.

The objects of his devouring appetite were reflected in the mirrors. Wherever he looked he saw, against a background of black satin, the fairest and whitest of all possible bodies, its dazzling sheen enhanced by the contrast of colours. Thighs round, firm and plump, an admirable fall of the loins, a . . . but I am obliged to respect the false delicacy of our language. Enough to say that our philosopher tasted again and again that portion of happiness which he was capable of tasting, and that the young Georgian very quickly became his 'sufficing reason'.

'Ah, Master, dear Master Pangloss!' Candide exclaimed in rapture, 'here everything is as good as in El Dorado. Nothing but a fine woman can satisfy a man's desires. I am as happy as it is possible to be. Leibnitz is right, and you, too, are a great philosopher.

'For instance,' he continued, addressing himself to the Georgian, 'I'll answer for it that you, my lovely girl, have always had a bias towards optimism, because you have always been happy.'

'Alas, no', she answered. 'I do not know what optimism is, but I swear to you that your slave has not known happiness before today. If his lordship is pleased to give me leave, I will convince him of this by a brief account of my past life.'

'With all my heart', said Candide. 'I am in a proper state of tranquillity to listen to a story.'

CHAPTER VII

ZIRZA'S STORY

'My father was a Christian,' said the Georgian, 'and I am one also, or so he told me. He had a little hermitage near Cotatis, where he gained the veneration of the faithful by his fervent devotion and by practising austerities shocking to human nature. Crowds of women came to pay him homage, and took a particular satisfaction in bathing his backside, which he would daily lacerate with blows. Doubtless it is to one of the most devout of these females that I owe my existence.

'I was brought up in a subterranean cave near my father's

cell. I was twelve years old, and had never left this tomb—as it may be called—when one day the earth shook with a dreadful noise, the roof of the cave fell in, and I was drawn out half dead from the rubble. Thus for the first time I saw the light of day.

'My father took me into his hermitage, as a child guarded by Providence for some special destiny. The people marvelled at my escape: my father cried it up as a miracle, and so did they.

'I was named Zirza, which in Persian means "Child of Providence". Notice was soon taken of my poor and scanty charms. Women came to the hermitage more seldom, men much more often. One of them declared that he loved me. "Villain," said my father, "hast thou that with which to love her? The child is a treasure entrusted to me by God. He appeared to me this night in the form of a venerable hermit, and forbade me to part with her for less than a thousand sequins. Get thee hence, wretch! Beware lest thy foul breath should blight her charms."

'"I have nothing to offer but my heart", said my suitor. "But say, barbarian, dost thou not blush to make a mockery of God for the gratification of thy greed? With what face, vile creature, darest thou to pretend that God has spoken to thee? To represent the Author of Beings as conversing with such men as thou art, is to mock him."

'"O blasphemy!", cried my father in a rage. "God himself has commanded to stone blasphemers." He flew at my unhappy suitor and with repeated blows laid him dead upon the ground. His blood was spirted in my face.

'Although I did not yet know what love is, this man had interested me, and his death threw me into a state of affliction, which was so much the worse as it made the sight of my father insupportable to me. I resolved to leave him, and he somehow perceived my design. "Ungrateful wench," says he, "it is to me thou owest thy being, thou art my daughter—and thou hatest me! But I am now going to deserve thy hatred, by using thee most rigorously."

'He kept his word but too well, cruel man! During five years, which I spent in tears and groans, neither my youth nor the fading of my beauty could abate his wrath. Sometimes he would thrust pins into all parts of my body; at other times he would make my backside all bloody with his whipping—'

'But that, I suppose, gave you less pain than the pins', said Candide.

'True, my Lord. . . At last I fled from the paternal dwelling. Having nobody in whom I dared to confide, I took to the woods, where I was for three days without food. I should have died of hunger but for a tiger who luckily took a fancy to me and was willing to let me share in his prey. But I had many horrors to endure from this formidable beast, who came very near to depriving me of that flower which your lordship has now plucked from me to my so great pain and pleasure.

'I took scurvy from the ill diet. When I was recovered from this I joined company with a merchant of slaves who was going to Tiflis. The plague was there then, and I caught it. These various misfortunes, however, did not utterly spoil my looks, nor prevent the Sophi's purveyor from buying me for your use.

'During the three months that I have been among the number of your women, I have languished in tears. My companions and I imagined ourselves to be the objects of your scorn; and if your lordship knew what miserable creatures eunuchs are, and how little adapted for comforting young girls who are scorned. . .

'In short, I am not yet eighteen years of age, and of these I have spent twelve in a dreadful dungeon. I have been in an earthquake. I have been splashed with the blood of the first tolerable man whom I saw. For four years I endured the most cruel tortures. I have had scurvy and the plague. Finally, I have spent three months in this seraglio amidst a crew of black and white monstrosities, still retaining that which I saved from the fury of an uncouth tiger, and cursing my fate. I should have died of the jaundice had not your Excellency honoured me at last with his embraces.'

'Good Heavens,' said Candide, 'is it possible that one of your tender age should have suffered such bitter woes? What would Pangloss say, if he could hear you? But your misfortunes are ended, as mine are. Everything is not too bad, now—or how think you?'

Candide thereupon resumed his caresses, and became every minute a stauncher supporter of the doctrines of Pangloss.

CHAPTER VIII

THE ABBÉ AGAIN

SETTLED in the midst of his seraglio, Candide shared out his favours to all, enjoying the pleasures of variety, but returning always with fresh ardour to the 'Child of Providence'.

But this did not last long. He soon began to suffer from violent pains in the loins, and excruciating colics. His pursuit of pleasure seemed somehow to wither him up. Zirza's breasts began to seem less white and less well placed, her buttocks less firm and plump. Her eyes seemed to have lost their sparkle, her complexion its lustre and her lips the vivid redness that had once delighted him. He noticed that she carried herself badly and had an unpleasant smell. He was disgusted to observe a birthmark on her mount of

Venus, which he had formerly thought free from blemish. Her ardours became a nuisance.

As his desires cooled, he found in his other women faults that he had not before perceived. He began to see nothing in them but a shameful lewdness. He became ashamed to have followed in the steps of the wisest of men, *et invenit amariorem morte mulierem.*

Pondering these truly Christian sentiments, Candide was one day occupying his leisure by walking in the streets of Sus, when a superbly dressed cavalier addressed him by name and embraced him. 'Can it be possible?' Candide stuttered. 'Can you, my Lord, be . . . no, it is not possible . . . yet you so much resemble . . . Monsieur l'Abbé from Perigord.'

'Yes, indeed, I am he', said the abbé.

Candide recoiled three paces. 'Tell me, Monsieur l'Abbé,' he said simply, 'are you happy?'

'My dear sir, need you ask?' said the abbé, and proceeded to relate his most recent adventures. 'The little deceit which I put upon you,' he said, 'contributed not a little to bring me into credit. The police employed me for some time; but I fell out with them, and quitted the priestly habit, which was no longer of any advantage to me.

'I then went over into England, where persons of my profession are better paid. I said all that I knew, and much that I did not know, of the strength and weakness of the country I had forsaken. Above all, I insisted that the French were the dregs amongst the nations, and that good sense was to be found only in London.

'In short, I made a splendid fortune, and have just concluded a treaty with the Persian Court, by which the Sophi undertakes to exterminate all Europeans who, to the prejudice of the English, visit his dominions in quest of cotton or silk.'

'The object of your mission is doubtless very praise-worthy,' said Candide. 'But, Monsieur l'Abbé, you are a rascal. I do not like rascals, and I have some influence at Court. You may well tremble, for your good fortune is at an end. You shall suffer the fate you deserve.'

'My Lord Candide,' said the abbé, throwing himself upon his knees, 'have mercy! I feel that I am drawn to evil by an irresistible force, in the same manner as you are impelled to virtue. I have perceived in myself this fatal bent ever since I became acquainted with Monsieur Valsp and worked at the *Feuilles*.'

'What are the *Feuilles*?'

'They are pamphlets of seventy-two pages, which enter-tain the public with calumny, satire and scurrility. Their inventor was a person whose worthy qualifications for the task were that he knew how to read and write, could not remain a Jesuit as long as he would have wished, and sought the wherewithal to buy his wife lace and bring up his children in the fear of God. He is assisted by some other honest fellows in return for a few halfpence and a few pints of bad wine.

'This Monsieur Valsp is also a member of a very facetious club, who divert themselves with making people drunk and inducing them to blaspheme; or with bullying some poor devil, breaking his furniture and afterwards challenging him. Such pretty little amusements these gentry call "hoaxes"—and the police ought to know about them.

'In short, this excellent Monsieur Valsp—we have his own word for it that he was never in the galleys—suffers from an anæsthesia which renders him insensible even to the simplest and harshest truth. He can be cured of this only by certain violent methods, which he endures with a resignation and courage above all description.

'I worked for some time under this eminent writer,

until I became an eminent writer in my turn. I had just quitted Monsieur Valsp, to set up for myself, when I had the honour of paying you a visit at Paris.'

'You are a great rogue, Monsieur l'Abbé, but I am touched by your sincerity. Go to court and ask for the Reverend Ed-Ivan-Baal-Denk. I shall write to him in your behalf—on condition that you promise to become an honest man, and that you will not encompass the murder of thousands of people for the sake of a little silk and cotton.'

The abbé gave the required promises, and they parted amicably.

CHAPTER IX

CANDIDE IS DISGRACED

ONCE at court, the abbé used all his skill to win the favour of the Prime Minister and to ruin his benefactor. With the latter object he spread a rumour that Candide had committed High Treason by speaking irreverently of the Sophi's whiskers. The courtiers urged that Candide should be roasted over a slow fire. The Sophi, with more humanity, sentenced him only to perpetual banishment.

Persian custom decreed that before his departure Candide should kiss his accuser's feet. The abbé himself travelled to Sus to enforce this part of the sentence. He found Candide in more or less restored health and inclined once more to an optimistic outlook. 'My dear friend,' said England's emissary, 'I come with regret to let you know that you must leave the Empire at once—and that first you must kiss my feet, with true repentance for your enormous misdeeds.'

'Kiss your feet, Monsieur l'Abbé!' said Candide, 'I do not understand such jokes.' Thereupon some deaf-mutes who had come from court with the abbé entered the room and removed the latter's shoes, indicating to Candide by signs that he must submit to the prescribed humiliation, or be impaled. Candide, making exercise of his Free Will, kissed the abbé's feet. He was then dressed in sack-cloth and driven out of the city by the public executioner, who repeatedly called out: 'A traitor, a traitor! He has spoken irreverently of the Sophi's Whiskers! Irreverently of the Imperial Whiskers!'

Meanwhile what was Ed-Ivan-Baal-Denk, that influential cenobite, doing whilst his protégé was being thus maltreated? I do not know. Probably he was tired of protecting Candide. Who can rely on the favour of princes, and how much less on that of monks?

Candide disconsolately went his way. 'I never even mentioned the King's whiskers', he reflected. 'Yet in a moment I am cast down from the peak to the abyss of fortune; and all because a wretch who has himself broken every known law brings a false accusation against me. Meanwhile this wretch, this monster, this persecutor of virtue—*he* achieves happiness!'

After travelling on foot for several days Candide reached the Turkish frontier, and proceeded in the direction of the Propontis, intending to settle there for good and to spend the rest of his days digging in his garden.

While passing through a small town, he found its population in an uproar. An elderly passer-by told him the reason for the excitement. Some time before the wealthy Mehemet had married the daughter of the Janissary Zamoud, and had found that she was not a virgin. Naturally enough, and with full legal right, he disfigured her face and sent her back to her father. Zamoud, equally naturally, was furious at this affront, and drawing his scimitar cut off the head of his disfigured daughter. His eldest son, who—and this again was entirely natural—loved his sister deeply, flew at his father and plunged a sharp dagger in his belly. After this the younger Zamoud—like a lion enraged by the sight of blood—rushed off to Mehemet's house, where, after cutting down some slaves who tried to stop him, he massacred Mehemet, his wives, and two of his children who were in their cradles: all of which was very natural, seeing that he was in such a violent rage. He concluded the episode by killing himself with the dagger reeking with his father's and his enemies' blood.

'O horrible!' exclaimed Candide. 'Ah, Master Pangloss, what would you say to such barbarities in nature? Surely you would acknowledge that nature is corrupted, that after all everything is *not*—'

'No,' said the elderly stranger, 'for the pre-established harmony—'

'Ah, Heavens, do ye not deceive me? Is it Pangloss that I see?'

'The very same. I recognized you, but I had a mind to penetrate into your sentiments before I discovered myself. Come, let us discourse a little on contingent effects, and see if you have made any progress in the art of wisdom.'

'Faith, this is no time for such a discussion. Rather tell me what is become of Cunégonde and the others.'

'I know nothing of them. It is two years since I left our dwelling in search of you. I have travelled over almost all Turkey, and was on the point of setting out for the Court of Persia, where I heard you made a great figure. I was tarrying in this little town, among these good people, only to gather strength for continuing my journey.'

'But what do I see? You have lost an arm!'

'It is of no consequence. Nothing is more common in this best of worlds than to see persons who want both an eye and an arm. I met with this misfortune in a journey from Mecca. Our caravan was attacked by Arabs. Our guards attempted to make resistance, thus giving the Arabs, who happened to be the stronger, the right, in accordance with the usages of war, to massacre us all. Some five hundred persons were killed, among them about a dozen women with child.

'For my part, I had only my skull split and an arm cut off. I did not die of it, and have maintained my belief that everything happened for the best.

'But what of yourself, my dear Candide? Whence have you that wooden leg?'

Candide gave an account of his adventures, and the two philosophers returned to the Propontis, enlivening their journey with discussions on physical and moral evil, free will and pre-destination, monads and the pre-established harmony.

CHAPTER X

PANGLOSS AND THE OFFICER

'AH, Candide, why did you grow tired of digging in your garden?' said Pangloss. 'Why could we not be content with our candied citrons and pistachios? Why were you bored by your happiness?

'There was, of course, a necessity—since everything in this best of worlds is necessary—that you should suffer the bastinado, and also have your leg cut off, the purpose being doubtless that you should make Chusistan happy, should learn the ingratitude of mankind, and should bring down upon some villains a deserved punishment.'

Conversing in this fashion they arrived at their old home, where they found Martin and Paquette clothed as slaves. After affectionately embracing them Candide inquired the reason for this metamorphosis.

'Alas,' said Martin, 'you no longer have any house of your own. Another is entrusted with the digging of your garden, he eats your citrons and your pistachios, and treats us like negroes.'

'Who is this interloper?'

'The High Admiral, the cruellest of men. The Sultan, who wished to reward his services without cost to himself, has confiscated all your goods, under pretext that you had gone over to his enemies, and has condemned us to slavery.

'Take my advice, Candide, and proceed on your way. I have always told you that everything is for the worst, and that the sum of evil far exceeds the sum of good. Go your way, and I do not despair but you may become a Manichæan, if you are not already.'

Candide interrupted Pangloss's inevitable protests by asking for news of Cunégonde and the others—the old woman, Friar Giroflée and Cacambo.

'Cacambo is here', said Martin. 'He is at present occupied in cleaning out a sewer. The old woman is dead of a kick in the stomach given her by a eunuch. Friar Giroflée has enlisted with the Janissaries. Mistress Cunégonde has recovered her plumpness and former beauty: she is in our master's seraglio.'

'What a chain of misfortunes!' said Candide. 'Was it then necessary that Cunégonde should again become beautiful, only to make me a cuckold?'

'It is of little consequence', said Pangloss, 'whether Mistress Cunégonde be beautiful or ugly, or whether she be in your arms or another's—all this is nothing to the general system. For my part, I wish her a numerous posterity. Philosophers do not concern themselves to know by whom women have children, provided they have them. The whole question of population—'

'Philosophers', said Martin, 'ought much rather to

employ themselves in rendering a few individuals happy, than in inciting the suffering species to multiply itself.'

At this moment they heard a sudden hubbub. The High Admiral was amusing himself by having a dozen slaves whipped. Pangloss and Candide were terrified. They sorrowfully parted from their friends and set out in haste for Constantinople.

They found the capital in consternation. Fire had broken out in the suburb of Pera, and had already consumed five or six hundred houses and killed from two to three thousand people. 'What a disaster!' said Candide.

'All is for the best', said Pangloss. 'These little accidents happen every year. Houses built of wood naturally catch fire, and are naturally burnt down. Besides, this means deliverance for a number of good people who have hitherto languished in poverty—'

'What is this I hear?' said an officer of the Sublime Porte. 'How, wretch, darest thou say that all is for the best, when half Constantinople is in flames? Go, dog, cursed of the Prophet, receive the punishment due to thy presumption!' He took Pangloss by the waist and threw him into the flames. Candide, numb with terror, crept to another district, where things were quieter.

CHAPTER XI

CANDIDE AND THE LAPP WIFE

'My only choice', said Candide, 'is of becoming a slave, or turning Turk. Happiness has forsaken me for ever.

'A turban would corrupt all my pleasures. I could find no peace of mind in a religion full of imposture, and one more-over which I should have embraced only from base self-interest. No, I shall never be at ease if I cease to be an honest man. I shall be a slave.'

He chose as his master an Armenian merchant, a good-natured man who was generally reputed to be as honest as an Armenian can be. He paid Candide two hundred sequins for his liberty.

The Armenian happened at this time to be setting out for Norway. He took Candide with him, hoping that a philosopher would be useful in his business. With favourable winds, the passage took only half the usual time. They did not even need to buy wind from the Lapland sorcerers—to whom, however, they made some small gifts, to prevent them from spoiling the luck with spells: which these people can do, if one is to believe Moréri's Dictionary.

On arrival the Armenian bought a stock of blubber and ordered Candide to travel about the country buying stock-fish. Candide did his best, and eventually started back for the trading-station with several reindeer-loads of this commodity.

As he was lodging for a night with a Lapp family, he had opportunity to observe the remarkable difference between Lapland customs and those of other nations. The woman of the house—a tiny creature with a head slightly bigger than the rest of her body, red eyes, a flat nose and an enormous mouth—greeted him with great composure and grace. 'My little Lord,' she said—her height was twenty-two inches—'I think you very handsome, pray be so kind as to love me a little.' She jumped up and flung her arms round his neck.

Candide pushed her away in disgust. She screamed, and her husband entered with several other Lapps. 'What is the meaning of this uproar?' he said.

'This stranger,' said the little creature, '—alas, I am choked with grief—he scorns me.'

'So that is it!' said the husband. 'Thou uncivil, dishonest, brutal, base, cowardly rascal, thou hast brought shame upon my household, thou hast done me the most deadly insult—thou refusest to lie with my wife.'

'Why, here's a fellow for you!' said Candide. 'What would you have said if I had lain with her?'

'I should have wished thee all manner of prosperity. But now thou deservest only my anger.' He began striking Candide across the back with a cudgel.

The relations of the aggrieved husband seized the reindeer. Candide fled, in fear that worse might occur. He had to give up all prospect of seeing his good master again, for he dared not appear before him with no whale-blubber, no stockfish and no reindeer.

CHAPTER XII

THE NEWTONIANS AND THE PARRICIDE

CANDIDE wandered aimlessly for some time, and then decided to go to Denmark, where he had heard that everything was pretty good. He had a little money which the Armenian had given him, and hoped that it would last out to the end of the journey. He was fortified against hardships and penury by hopes of the future, and was still, on the whole, fairly cheerful.

One day, while staying at an inn, he heard three travellers in eager discussion, during which he caught the words 'plenum' and 'materia subtilis'. 'This is excellent,' he thought, and decided to join in. 'Gentlemen,' he said, 'a plenum is incontestable: there is no vacuum in Nature, and the materia subtilis is a well-imagined hypothesis.'

'You are a Cartesian, then?' said one of the travellers.

'Yes, and a Leibnitzian, which is more.'

'So much the worse for you', said traveller Number Two. 'Descartes and Leibnitz were dolts. We are Newtonians, and proud of it. If we dispute, it is only to confirm ourselves in our opinions, for we all think alike. We seek for the truth in Newton's footsteps, for we are persuaded that Newton is a great man.'

'So is Descartes, and Leibnitz, and Pangloss, too,' said Candide. 'These great men are worth a heap of others.'

'You are a presumptuous fool, my friend', said traveller Number Three. 'Do you know the laws of refraction, attraction and motion? Have you read Dr. Clark's refutation of your Leibnitz's rubbish? Do you know the meaning of the expressions "centrifugal" and "centripetal force"? Have you any notion of the theory of light, or of gravitation? Are you familiar with the period of twenty-five thousand, nine hundred and twenty years, which unfortunately upsets the established chronology?

'No, for certain you are utterly ignorant of all these things. Hold your peace, then, puny monad, and beware how you insult giants by comparing them to pygmies.'

'If Pangloss were here, gentlemen,' said Candide, 'he would set you to rights, for he is a great philosopher. He has a sovereign contempt for your Newton. Therefore I, as his pupil, also hold Newton in little esteem.'

At this the three travellers fell upon Candide and thrashed him with philosophic ferocity. Afterwards their wrath subsided, and they begged Candide to pardon their warmth of feeling. Traveller Number One made an excellent speech on the beauty of mildness and moderation.

An elaborate funeral passed by the inn, and caused the four philosophers to comment on the foolish vanity of man. 'Would it not be more reasonable', said traveller Number Two, 'that the relations and friends of the deceased should in all simplicity carry the bier themselves? Surely this funeral act, by reminding them of death, would produce a most salutary and philosophical effect. "This body that I carry", a man might say, " is that of my friend, my relation. He is no more; and I, like him, must cease to be." Such a reflection might well save this unhappy globe from many a crime, and bring back to virtue those beings who believe in the immortality of the soul.

'Men are all too apt to keep the thought of death at a distance, and there is therefore no danger of its becoming too strongly present in their minds. Why, then, are weeping wives and mothers led away from the spectacle of death? The plaintive accents of nature, the piercing cries of despair, would do much greater honour to the ashes of the dead than all these individuals clad in black from head to foot, these useless female mourners, or all the officiating clergy chanting funeral orations that they themselves do not understand.'

'Well said', Candide answered. 'Did you always speak so well, without thinking proper to thrash people, you would be a great philosopher.'

Parting on friendly terms with the three Newtonians, Candide continued his journey towards Denmark. Whilst passing through a forest he began thinking of all the misfortunes that had befallen him in this best of worlds. The result was that he strayed from the high road and lost himself.

It was dusk when he noticed his error. In dismay he raised his eyes to Heaven, leaned against the trunk of a tree and soliloquized as follows: 'I have travelled over half the globe; I have seen deceit and slander triumphant; I have sought only to do service to mankind, and I have been sorely persecuted. A great king honours me with his favour, and with fifty strokes of a bull's pizzle. I arrive, with a wooden leg, in a very fine province: there, after drinking deep of gall and grief, I taste a few pleasures. An abbé comes,

I protect him, he makes use of me to insinuate himself at court—and the result is that I am obliged to kiss his feet. . . . I meet with my poor Pangloss, only to see him burnt. I find myself in company with philosophers, the mildest and most sociable of all animals, and they beat me unmercifully. . . . All must be for the best, since Pangloss has said it, but nonetheless I am the most unhappy of beings.'

His meditations were interrupted by piercing cries from near by, and he went to find the reason for them. A young woman was tearing her hair in anguish. 'Whoever you are,' she said, 'if you have a heart, follow me.' They walked together for a few yards, and Candide saw a man and woman stretched on the ground. Their faces revealed a nobility both of spirit and of birth, and their features, although distorted by pain, had in them something so interesting that Candide felt a pang of deep compassion. He anxiously asked what had caused their plight. 'They are my father and mother,' said the young woman, '—yes, the authors of my unhappy being. They were in flight from a harsh and unjust sentence, and I accompanied them, happy to share in their misfortunes, with the sweet hope that in the wilds where we would hide ourselves my feeble hands might procure them a necessary subsistence.

'We stopped here to take some rest, and I found that tree yonder. Its fruit deceived me. . . . Ah, sir, I am a thing of horror to the universe and to myself! Draw, then, to avenge outraged virtue and to punish parricide—strike! . . . This fruit, I gave it to my father and mother. They ate of it with pleasure. I rejoiced to have found the means of quenching the thirst with which they were tormented. . . . Unhappy wretch, it was death I gave them: this fruit is poison!'

Candide shuddered, his hair crisped up, and he came out in a cold sweat. He longed to do anything he could to help this unlucky family; but the poison had already made too much progress, and the best antidotes would have been useless.

'Dear child, our only hope,' said the father, 'forgive thyself, as we forgive thee. It was thy excessive love that has slain us.'

'Noble stranger,' said the mother, 'vouchsafe to take care of her. Her heart is noble and formed for virtue. 'Tis a treasure that we commit to your care, infinitely more precious than the fortune which we once had. . . .'

'Dear Zenoida,' said the father, 'receive our last embrace, mingle thy tears with ours. Ah, Heaven, let us remember that this is truly a time for rejoicing! The door of the dark dungeon where we have languished for forty years is now flung open.'

'Sweet Zenoida,' said the mother, 'receive our blessing. Mayst thou never forget the lessons which our years have taught thee, and may they preserve thee from the abyss that we see before thy feet!'

Soon afterwards both parents died. Zenoida passed into a swoon, from which Candide had difficulty in recovering her. The moonlit night had given place to dawn before she came to her senses. As soon as she opened her eyes, she asked Candide to dig a grave for the bodies, and with astonishing fortitude herself helped in the work. This duty done, she allowed herself to weep.

Candide was eager to remove Zenoida as soon as possible from the scene of the disaster. They walked on at random until they came to a small cottage. Its owners were an aged couple who, as dwellers in the wilds, were always ready to give all the help they could to fellow-creatures in distress. These old people were like the legendary Philemon and Baucis. For fifty years they had enjoyed the pleasures of wedlock without ever experiencing its bitterness. Robust health—the result of temperate living and quiet minds; an inexhaustible fund of honesty and simplicity; and all the other virtues that man owes only to himself: these were Heaven's only dowry upon their marriage. They were venerated in the neighbouring villages, whose inhabitants might—had they been Catholics—have been considered very decent people. The villagers made a point of never letting Agaton and Sunama—these were the old couple's names—want for anything; and their charity extended itself to the newcomers.

'Ah, Pangloss,' thought Candide, 'what a great pity it is that you were burnt. You were certainly in the right. Nevertheless, your doctrine that "everything is for the best" does not hold good in all the parts of Europe and Asia that you and I have visited together; but only in El Dorado, where nobody can go, and in a little cottage situated in a cold, barren and harsh region.

'How delightful it would be, my dear Pangloss,' Candide mused absently, 'if you were here, too, to discourse of the pre-established harmony and the monads. . . . I should be very willing to spend all my days among these honest Lutherans. . . . But then I should have to give up going to Mass, and be torn to pieces in the *Journal Chrétien*.'

Candide was very curious to know Zenoida's history, but consideration for her feelings prevented him from asking questions. She realized this, and spontaneously told him her story.

CHAPTER XIII

ZENOIDA'S STORY

'I AM descended', said Zenoida, 'from one of the oldest families in Denmark. One of my ancestors perished at the banquet where the wicked King Christian contrived the death of so many senators.

'The riches and honours amassed by my family have served only to render their misfortunes more illustrious. My father had the hardiness to displease a great man by telling him the truth. Suborned accusers brought false charges against him. His judges were deceived—what judge can always detect the snares that calumny spreads for innocence? My father, being sentenced to the scaffold, took refuge in the house of a friend—or rather, of one whom he thought deserving of that glorious title.

'We remained for some time concealed in a castle which this man possesses on the sea coast; and we might be there yet, had not the base wretch, taking advantage of our plight, attempted to repay himself for his services at a detestable price. The infamous monster had conceived an unnatural passion for my mother and myself, and attempted our virtue by methods most unworthy of a man of honour. To escape from his brutal passion we were compelled to face the dreadful dangers of a renewed flight. The rest you know.'

Zenoida wept anew. Candide wiped away her tears and said consolingly: 'Madam, everything is for the best. If your father had not died by poison, he would have infallibly have been discovered, and would have lost his head. Your mother would perhaps have died of grief, and you and I should not now be in this poor hovel, where everything is a great deal better than in the finest of castles.'

'Alas, sir, my father never told me that everything was for the best. We all belong to God, who loves us but has not exempted us from gnawing cares, cruel maladies and the innumerable ills that afflict the human race. In America poison and the quinquina grow side by side. Even the happiest mortal has known what it is to weep. A compound of pleasure and pain constitutes what we call life: that is to say, a set span of time, always too long in the sight of the wise, which we should employ in doing good to the community in which we are placed; in enjoying the works of the Almighty, without foolishly seeking after their hidden causes; in regulating our conduct by the biddings of our conscience; and, above all, in respecting religion—happy when, as but rarely, we can live up to it.

'All this is what my revered father used to tell me. "Unhappy are those rash and presumptuous writers", he would say, "who attempt to pry into the secrets of the Almighty." On the principle that God wishes to be honoured by the countless atoms to which he has given being, men have wedded respectable truths with absurd chimeras. The Dervish in Turkey, the Brahmin in India, the Bonze in China, the Talapoin in Burma, all these worship the Deity in a different way from ours: but amidst the darkness in which they are plunged they enjoy peace of soul. He who seeks to dispel this darkness would do them but an ill service. To pluck men from the realm of superstition is to do them no kindness.'

'You speak like a philosopher', said Candide. 'May I ask you, my fair lady, of what religion you are?'

'I was brought up in Lutheranism. It is the religion of my country.'

'Everything that you have said has been like a ray of light penetrating my soul. You fill me with esteem and admiration. . . . But how, in the name of wonder, came so bright an understanding to be lodged in so beautiful a form? Upon my word, Mistress, I esteem and admire you so much that . . .'

Candide stammered a few more words. Zenoida, perceiving his confusion, went away. From then on she tried to avoid being alone with him.

Candide, on the other hand, sought to be either alone with Zenoida or alone by himself. He was steeped in a melancholy not without charm. Although desperately in love, he tried to conceal his passion even from himself. His looks, however, betrayed his heart's secret. 'Ah me,' he would often say to himself, 'if Master Pangloss were here he would give me good advice, for he was a great philosopher.'

CHAPTER XIV

THE WOOING OF ZENOIDA

CANDIDE's only consolation was to converse with Zenoida in the presence of their hosts. 'How came it', he said to her one day, 'that the King, to whom you had access, could suffer such an injustice to be done to your family? You hate him, I'll be bound.'

'How!' said Zenoida. 'Who can hate their king? Who can feel anything but love for him to whom is entrusted the glittering blade of the law? Kings are the living images of the Deity, and we ought never to arraign their conduct. Obedience and respect are the duty of good subjects.'

'I admire your judgment more and more. Pray, Mistress, do you know the great Leibnitz, or the great Pangloss, who was burned after having escaped hanging? Are you acquainted with the monads, the *materia subtilis* and the vortices?'

'No, sir, I have never heard my father mention any of these. He gave me only a tincture of empirical philosophy, and taught me to hold in contempt all those kinds of philosophy that do not directly contribute to man's happiness; that give him false notions of his duty to himself and his neighbours; that do not teach him self-control; that fill his mind only with barbarous expressions and rash conjectures; or that fail to give him a clearer idea of the Author of Being than what he may acquire from His works and His wonders which are daily shown before our eyes.'

'I repeat, Madam, that you fill me with admiration. You enchant me, you ravish me, you an are angel that Heaven has sent to refute for me the sophisms of Master Pangloss.

'Ah, what a silly animal I was! I have been kicked on the backside, beaten with ramrods, bastinadoed with a bull's pizzle. I was in an earthquake. I saw Dr. Pangloss first hanged and later burnt. I was ravished in a most agonizing fashion by a villainous Persian. I was robbed by a decree of the Divan. I was thrashed by a set of philosophers—and yet I believed that everything was for the best! Now I am thoroughly undeceived.

'Nevertheless, Nature never seemed to me more lovely than since I have seen you. The rural concert of the birds has for me a harmony that I never knew before. The glow of sentiment that enchants me seems reflected in everything I see.

'I feel none of that soft languor which I felt in my gardens at Sus. The inspiration I get from you is wholly different.'

'Hold, hold!' said Zenoida. 'You seem to be running to lengths that might offend my delicacy, which you ought to respect.'

'I shall be silent, but my sentiments will be all the more ardent.' Candide looked steadily at Zenoida, who blushed. As a man of experience he thought this a good sign. The young Dane, however, continued to elude his advances.

One day, as Candide was pacing to and fro in the garden of the cottage, he exclaimed in amorous rapture: 'Ah, to think that I no longer have my El Dorado sheep! That I no longer have it in my power to purchase even a small kingdom! Why, if I were a king——'

'What should I be to you?' said a voice that pierced through Candide's heart.

''Tis you, lovely Zenoida!' he said, falling on his knees. 'I thought myself alone. The few words I just now heard you utter seem to promise me the bliss to which I aspire. I shall never be a king, perhaps I shall never even be rich. But, if you love me. . . . Do not turn from me those beauteous eyes, but let me read in them a confession which alone can make me happy.

'Lovely Zenoida, I adore you. Open your soul to pity. . . . What do I see? You weep! Ah, my good fortune is greater than I deserve. . . .'

'Yes, you have that good fortune', said Zenoida. 'There is no reason why I should disguise my feeling for a person I think deserving of it. Hitherto you have been attached to my destiny only by bonds of human kindness. It is time to reinforce these bonds with others more sacred. I have taken counsel with myself: do you, for your part, reflect maturely. Remember, above all, that in marrying me you become obliged to protect me—to sweeten and share with me those miseries that fate has still perhaps in store for me.'

'Marrying you!' said Candide. 'Those words have opened my eyes to the imprudence of my conduct. Alas, dear idol of my life, I am not deserving of your goodness. Cunégonde is yet living. . . .'

'Cunégonde—who is she?'

'My wife.'

For a few seconds neither lover could say a word. Weeping, they struggled for utterance. Candide took Zenoida's hands in his, pressed them against his heart and kissed them repeatedly. He made so bold as to raise his own hands to his beloved's bosom, and perceived that she was gasping for breath. His soul rose to his lips, and his lips pressed upon hers, bringing the young Danish beauty back from a trance.

He thought he could read forgiveness in her eyes. 'Dear

lover,' she said, 'I would do ill to repay with anger those transports to which my heart consents. Yet hold, you would ruin me in the opinion of the world—and you yourself would soon cease to love me, if once I became the object of contempt. Forbear, therefore, and spare my weakness.'

'How, because the stupid rabble say that a woman loses her honour by bestowing happiness upon a being whom she loves, and who loves her; by following that sweet natural bent which in the world's golden age. . . .'

It is sufficient to add that Candide's eloquence had all the effect that was to be expected upon a young, full-blooded female philosopher.

The days of melancholy and boredom were over, and the two lovers passed their time in a continual intoxication of delight. The glorious sap of amorous pleasure gushed through their veins. The silent forests, the mountains covered with briars and flanked by precipices, the frozen plains and the rugged fields, persuaded them more and more of their need to love. They resolved never to leave these frightful wastes.

But fate, as we shall see in the next chapter, had more persecutions in store for them.

CHAPTER XV

VOLHALL INTERVENES

CANDIDE and Zenoida discussed the works of the Deity; the worship that men owe Him; man's duty to his fellow; and especially charity—that most practical of all the virtues.

They were not content with empty words. Candide taught the boys of the neighbourhood to respect the sacred bonds of law. Zenoida taught the girls their duty to their parents. Together they sowed in these young hearts the prolific seeds of religion.

One day Sunama came to tell Zenoida that an old gentleman with a large following of servants had arrived at the cottage looking for a person who, from his description, was undoubtedly Zenoida herself. The gentleman followed close on Sunama's heels, and, before she could close the door, had entered the young couple's room.

Zenoida fainted at the sight of him. But Volhall—this was the old man's name—relentlessly seized her by the hand and pulled her to her feet so violently that she recovered consciousness; whereupon she burst into tears.

'So, niece,' said Volhall, with a sardonic smile, 'I find you in fine company. I do not wonder that you prefer it to life in the capital, to my home and to your family.'

'Yes, sir,' said Zenoida, 'I do prefer the dwelling of simplicity and truth to the mansions of treachery and imposture. I can never behold but with horror that place where my misfortunes began; where I had so many proofs of the blackness of your heart; and where I have no other relations but yourself.'

'Come, madam,' said Volhall, 'follow me, if you please; for so you shall, even if you should faint again.' He dragged her out of the cottage and thrust her into a waiting carriage. She had time only to bid Candide follow after her, to bless her hosts and to promise them reward for their generous hospitality. Then the carriage drove off.

One of Volhall's servants took pity on Candide's despair. Supposing that his interest in Zenoida came merely from sympathy with virtue in distress, the servant advised him to travel to Copenhagen, and gave him directions for the journey. Furthermore, he suggested that, if Candide had no other means of livelihood, he might be taken on as one of Volhall's servants.

Candide thought this an excellent suggestion. When he reached Copenhagen the servant who had befriended him presented him to Volhall as one of his relations, for whom he could answer.

'Rascal,' said Volhall to Candide, 'I grant you the honour of waiting on such a person as myself. Never forget the profound respect that you owe to my wishes. You must, indeed, anticipate them, if you have the wits to do so. Reflect constantly that a man of my quality degrades himself even in speaking to a creature like you.'

Candide replied submissively, and the same day assumed his new master's livery.

It is easy to imagine Zenoida's surprise and joy when she recognized her lover among her uncle's servants. She contrived various opportunities, which Candide adroitly took. They swore unshakable fidelity.

Zenoida had her faults. Sometimes she felt ashamed of her love for Candide, and sometimes she vexed him with her caprices. But Candide adored her, and knew that no man, and still less any woman, can be perfect. In his arms Zenoida would recover her good humour. The constraint upon them made their moments of pleasure all the more exciting: they were still happy.

CHAPTER XVI

THE JEALOUS CUNÉGONDE

CANDIDE's only hardship in this new life was his master's haughtiness; and this was a cheap price to pay for the favours of his mistress.

Unfortunately, happy lovers cannot conceal their doings as easily as is sometimes supposed. Candide and Zenoida soon gave themselves away, and their connection was no longer a secret from anyone in the household except Volhall. Candide's fellow-servants scared him with their overt congratulations: he felt sure that disaster was impending.

He did not suspect, however, that this disaster would be hastened on by a person who had once been dear to him. For several days he had from time to time noticed in the streets a woman who resembled Cunégonde. Then, one day he saw this woman in the courtyard of Volhall's house. She was very poorly dressed, and there seemed to be no likelihood that the favourite of a rich Mahomedan should appear in a courtyard in Copenhagen. Nevertheless, this disagreeable object, after staring hard at Candide, came up and, seizing him by the hair, gave him a violent box on the ear.

'So it *is* you!' Candide exclaimed. 'Heavens, who would have thought it? What seek you here, you who have suffered yourself to be ravished by a follower of Mahomet? Go, faithless wife, I know you not.'

'Thou shalt know me by my fury', said Cunégonde. 'I am acquainted with the life thou leadest, thy love for thy master's niece and thy contempt for me.

'Alas, it is now three months since I quitted the seraglio, because I was no longer of any use in that place. A merchant bought me to mend his linen, and took me with him on a voyage to these coasts. Martin, Cacambo and Paquette— all of whom he also bought—are with us. Doctor Pangloss, by the strangest of chances, was a passenger on the same ship. We were shipwrecked some miles from hence. I escaped from drowning, together with the faithful Cacambo —who, I swear to thee, has a skin as fine as thy own.

'Now I find thee again, and find thee false. Tremble, then, with fear of an injured wife.'

Candide was so dazed by this touching scene that he

allowed Cunégonde to go, without reflecting how necessary it is to take precautions in dealing with any person who knows one's secrets.

Soon afterwards Cacambo entered the courtyard. Candide and he embraced affectionately. Candide inquired into the truth of what Cunégonde had told him, and was deeply distressed to learn that Pangloss—after escaping from the gallows and the flames—had in fact been drowned.

They were talking like old friends, when Zenoida threw a small *billet* from a window. Candide opened it, and read as follows:

'Fly, my dear Lover: all is discovered. An innocent propensity, which Nature authorizes, and does no injury to society, is a crime in the eyes of superstitious and cruel men. Volhall has just left my chamber, after treating me with the utmost inhumanity: he is gone to obtain an order to throw you into prison, there to perish. Fly, my alas! too dear Lover: preserve a life which thou canst not pass any longer near me. Those happy hours are no more, in which our mutual tenderness. . . . Ah! wretched Zenoida, how hast thou offended Heaven, to meet so rigorous a fate? But I wander: remember always thy loving Zenoida. Dear Lover, thou shalt live eternally within my heart. . . . No, thou hast never known how much I loved thee . . . O that thou couldst receive upon my burning lips my last adieu, and catch my last sigh! I am ready to follow my unhappy father. The light of day is hateful to me: it shines but upon villainies.'

Cacambo, quick-witted and practical as ever, took Candide—who was almost out of his mind—by the arm, and led him from the city. Not until they were several miles from Copenhagen did Candide open his mouth. Then, rousing himself from his lethargy and staring at Cacambo, he spoke as follows.

CHAPTER XVII

CANDIDE MEDITATES SUICIDE

'Dear Cacambo, formerly my valet, now my equal and always my friend, thou hast had a share in some of my misfortunes, thou hast given me salutary advice, and thou has beheld my love for Mistress Cunégonde.'

'Alas, my former master!' said Cacambo, 'it is she who has played you a most scurvy trick. When she learnt from your fellow servants that you loved Zenoida, and that your love was requited, she revealed all to fierce Volhall.'

'If this be so, I have nothing more to do but die.' Candide brought out a knife, and began whetting it with a coolness worthy of an ancient Roman or an Englishman.

'What are you going to do?' Cacambo asked.

'To cut my throat.'

'There is no harm in contemplating such a step', said Cacambo quickly. 'But a wise man does not actually take it without mature deliberation. You can kill yourself at any time, should you wish to do so. Be advised by me, dear master, and put it off until tomorrow. The longer you defer the act itself, the more courageous will it be.'

'I am persuaded by thy reasoning. Besides, if I should cut my throat immediately, the *Journal de Trévoux* would insult my memory. It is agreed, then, that I shall not kill myself till two or three days hence.'

They arrived at Elsinore, a town of some size not far from Copenhagen. Here they put up at an inn. Next morning Cacambo noticed with pleasure that Candide had benefited greatly from a good night's rest. They left the town at daybreak.

Candide, still the philosopher—for habits acquired in youth are unbreakable—held forth to Cacambo about physical good and evil, the wise sayings of Zenoida and the truths he had imbibed from her conversation. 'God keep me', he said, 'from becoming a Manichæan. My mistress taught me to respect the impenetrable veil with which the Deity envelops his works among us.

'Perhaps mankind is itself responsible for its downfall into the pit of misery where now it groans. Of a frugivorous animal, man has made himself a carnivore. The savages whom we encountered in America eat only Jesuits, and live at peace with one another. And those other savages—if there are any such—who live scattered through the woods, living on acorns and herbs, are doubtless still more happy.

'To what crimes human society has given birth! There are men in this society who are compelled by their condition to desire the death of others. The shipwreck of a vessel, the burning of a house, the loss of a battle, cause sorrow in one quarter and joy in another.

'Everything is very bad, my dear Cacambo, and there is nothing left for a philosopher but to cut his throat as painlessly as possible.'

'You are in the right', said Cacambo. 'But I perceive a tavern, and you must be very thirsty. Come, my old master, let us take a glass, and after that we will continue our philosophical disquisitions.'

In the tavern yard they saw a company of peasants dancing to the music of some wretched instruments. They were all smiling, and the scene was worthy of the brush of Watteau. A young woman took Candide by the hand and invited him to dance with her. 'My pretty maid,' said Candide, 'when a man has lost his mistress, found his wife again, and heard that the great Pangloss is dead, he is in no mood to cut capers. Besides, I am to kill myself tomorrow morning; and you understand that a man who has but a few hours to live ought not to waste them in dancing.'

'The great philosophers', Cacambo interposed, 'always thirsted for distinction from their fellow-men. Cato of Utica killed himself after a nap. Socrates swallowed hemlock after diverting himself with his friends. Several Englishmen have blown their brains out after dinner. But I never yet heard of a great man who cut his throat after an agreeable dance. It is for you, my dear master, that this distinction is reserved. Take my advice, let us dance our fill, and we will kill ourselves tomorrow.'

'Have you not remarked', said Candide, 'that yonder young peasant girl is a very pretty brunette?'

'She has something very taking in her countenance', said Cacambo.

'She squeezed my hand.'

'Have you observed that in the hurry of the dance her kerchief has fallen aside, revealing two delightful little breasts?'

'Yes, I have observed that. Look you, if my heart were not filled with Mistress Zenoida . . .'

The brunette again approached Candide, and begged him to take one dance with her. He yielded to her persuasion, and danced with great skill and enjoyment. Then he kissed the young peasant and retired to his seat—without, unfortunately, having asked the Queen of the Ball to dance with him.

There was a general murmur. All the dancers and spectators were shocked at so flagrant a piece of disrespect. Candide was unaware that he had done anything wrong, and therefore could make no apology. A hulking rustic came up and hit him on the nose. Cacambo kicked the rustic in the belly. In a few seconds all the instruments had been broken and the women had lost their caps. Candide and Cacambo fought stubbornly, but were at length forced to take to their heels, bruised and bleeding.

'I am one for whom everything turns to poison', said Candide, giving Cacambo his arm. 'I have had many misfortunes, but I never expected to be beaten to a jelly for dancing with a country girl at her own request.'

CHAPTER XVIII

THE END OF PANGLOSS

CACAMBO and his one-time master felt hopeless and discouraged, and began to succumb to that spiritual sickness which numbs all the faculties. They came to a hospital built for wayfarers, and on Cacambo's suggestion entered it as patients.

They received the treatment usual in such places. That is to say, they were treated as non-paying patients—no further description is necessary. In a short time their wounds were healed, but they had caught the itch. This ailment, they found, was not easy to get rid of.

'Thou wouldst not let me cut my throat, my dear Cacambo', Candide remarked, scratching himself, with tears in his eyes. 'Thy ill advice has plunged me again in disgrace and misfortune. Were I to cut my throat now, the *Journal de Trévoux* would certainly say: "He was a coward, who killed himself because he had the itch". See to what thou hast brought me, with thy mistaken compassion.'

'Our woes are not without remedy', said Cacambo. 'If you will but please to listen to me, let us settle here as lay brothers. I understand a little surgery, and I promise to alleviate our sad condition and render it supportable.'

'The devil take all ignorant asses,' said Candide, 'and

especially all asses of surgeons, those perils to mankind. I shall not suffer thee to pretend to be what thou art not. I dread what such deceit might lead to.

'Besides, if thou didst but conceive how hard it is, after having once been Viceroy of a fine province, at another time rich enough to purchase kingdoms, at another time the favoured lover of Mistress Zenoida—after all this, to serve as a lay brother in a hospital . . .'

'I can conceive it to be hard. But I can also conceive that it is very hard to die of hunger. Bear in mind, moreover, that my proposal is perhaps your only means of eluding the search of the fierce Volhall, and the punishments he has in store for you.'

A lay brother of the hospital told them that the brethren enjoyed good living conditions and a reasonable amount of liberty. Candide was persuaded, and they applied for and at once received employment. Thus these two unfortunate beings began ministering to others like themselves.

One day, as Candide was distributing some thin, ill-tasting broth, he came upon an old man with a livid face, lips covered with froth, eyes half turned in his head and the image of death carved upon his lean and sunken cheeks. 'Poor man', said Candide. 'How I pity you! Your sufferings must be terrible.'

'Indeed they are', answered a sepulchral voice. 'They tell me that I am hectic, phthisical, asthmatic and poxed to the bone. If all that be true, I must be very ill indeed. Yet everything is good, and that is my consolation.'

'Why, none but Doctor Pangloss himself could come to so deplorable a plight and still maintain the doctrine of Optimism. Any other man in such a case would preach up Pess—'

'Do not speak that abominable word! I am that Pangloss you speak of. Everything is good, everything is for the best.'

The effort of pronouncing these words cost him his last tooth, which he spat out together with fragments of his corrupted lungs. A few moments later he died.

Candide mourned his death, for he had been a good-hearted man. The obstinacy with which he had clung to his beliefs caused Candide to think back over all the adventures they had been through together.

All this time, Cunégonde had remained in Copenhagen, where she had acquired, so Candide learnt, a great reputation as a mender of old clothes.

Candide had by now lost all taste for travelling. He had the friendship and good counsel of Cacambo, and he made no complaint against Providence. 'I know', he would say, 'that happiness is not the portion of man. Happiness dwells only in the good country of El Dorado, where nobody can go.'

CHAPTER XIX

THE LAST OF CUNÉGONDE

CANDIDE had not been too unfortunate, for he had found, in the person of a mestizo valet, something that a man may seek throughout Europe in vain: a true friend. Perhaps in America, where Nature has planted herbs that can heal the physical maladies of our continent, she may also have placed remedies for the maladies of our hearts and minds. Perhaps in this New World there are men altogether differently made from ourselves, men who are not slaves to self-interest, men worthy to carry the noble flame of friendship. How one could wish that, instead of indigo and cochineal —all stained with blood—the merchant vessels might bring us some of these men!

Cacambo was worth more to Candide than a dozen red sheep laden with the pebbles of El Dorado. Our philosopher once more began to take pleasure in the act of living. He found much comfort, also, in ministering to the preservation of human life, and in being a useful member of society. God rewarded the purity of his intentions by restoring to Cacambo and himself the joy of good health. They no longer had the itch, and could perform their unpleasant tasks with cheerfulness.

Fate, however, soon robbed them of this tranquillity and ease. Cunégonde had set her heart upon tormenting her husband, and left Copenhagen in search of him. She arrived, by pure chance, at the hospital, together with a man whom Candide recognized—with understandable astonishment—as the Baron von Thunder-ten-Tronckh.

The Baron explained how he came to be there. 'I was not kept long in the Ottoman galleys', he said. 'The Jesuits learned of my misfortune, and ransomed me for the honour of the Society. I then travelled to Germany, where I received some assistance from my father's heirs. I neglected no effort to find my sister, and had a message from Constantinople that she had sailed thence on a vessel which was shipwrecked on the coast of Denmark. I thereupon disguised myself, and obtained letters of recommendation to various Danish merchants who have correspondence with the Society.

'The upshot was that I found my sister. She still loves you—unworthy as you are of her regard—and since you have had the insolence to lie with her, I consent to the ratification of the marriage; or rather, to a new celebration of it. You understand, of course, that my sister shall give you only her left hand; which is very reasonable, since she has seventy-two quarterings, and you have not one.'

'Alas,' said Candide, 'all the quarterings in the world, without beauty ... Mistress Cunégonde was very ugly when I had the imprudence to marry her. Afterwards she became handsome again—and another enjoyed her charms. Now once again she is grown ugly—and you would have me give her my hand a second time. No, indeed, Reverend Father! Send her back to the seraglio on the Propontis. She has already done me too much mischief in this country.'

'Leave off, ungrateful wretch!' said Cunégonde, her face convulsed with fear and rage. 'Do not provoke the Herr Baron, who is a priest as well, to kill us both in order to wash out his disgrace with our blood.

'Dost thou believe me capable of having willingly failed in the fidelity I owed thee? What could I do against a man who was my master, and thought me handsome? Neither my tears nor my cries could soften his savage brutality. Seeing there was nothing to be done, I contrived to be ravished with the least inconvenience possible. Any other woman would have done the same.

'Such is all my crime: it does not deserve thy anger. A greater crime, in thy eyes, is having deprived thee of thy mistress. But this crime ought to convince thee of my love.

'Come, my darling, if ever I again become beautiful; if ever my bosom, that now droops and sags, should recover its firmness and elasticity; if—it will only be for thee, dear Candide. We are no longer in Turkey, and I swear faithfully to thee never to let myself be ravished again.'

This speech made little impression on Candide. He asked for a few hours in which to make up his mind. The Herr Baron granted him two hours, which he spent in consultation with Cacambo. After weighing the arguments *pro* and *con*, they decided to go with the Jesuit and his sister to Germany.

They set out from the hospital in a body—not on foot, but on good horses brought from Germany by the Baron. When they arrived at the Danish frontier, a big, villainous-looking fellow stared hard at Candide. 'It is the very man', he said, glancing at a little bit of paper. 'Sir, pardon my curiosity, is not your name Candide?'

'Yes, sir, that is my name.'

'You will be flattered to hear that your description does not belie you. You have, in very truth, black eyebrows, eyes neither sunken nor protruding, ears of middling size, a round, freshly coloured face; and it seems to me that you must be five feet five inches high.'

'Yes, sir, that is my height. But how are my ears and my height any concern of yours.'

'Sir, in our office we cannot be too circumspect. Permit me to ask you one more little question: were you not in the service of my Lord Volhall?'

'Indeed, sir, I do not understand. . . .'

'That may be, sir, but for my part I understand perfectly well that you are the person whose description has been sent to me. Please to walk into the guardroom. . . Men, take care of this gentleman, get the black hole ready, and send for the locksmith to make the gentleman a nice little chain of about thirty or forty pounds weight. Master Candide, you have a good horse there. I am in want of a horse of that colour. I dare say we shall agree about it.'

The Baron was afraid to say the horse was his. Candide was led off, and Cunégonde wept for fully fifteen minutes. The Jesuit was unperturbed. 'I should have been obliged to kill him, or to make him marry you over again', he said to his sister. 'All things considered, what has happened is much the best for the honour of our family.'

Cunégonde followed her brother back to Germany. Cacambo, however, would not forsake his friend.

CHAPTER XX

'EVERYTHING IS NOT TOO BAD'

'Ah, Pangloss,' sighed Candide, "tis pity you are dead. You were a witness of only a part of my misfortunes, and I hoped in time to have dissuaded you from that ill-founded opinion which you maintained to your last breath.

'No man has suffered more calamities than I. And yet, as the daughter of Pope Urban so well said, there is not a single person who has not many times cursed his existence. . .

'What is going to happen to me, Cacambo?' he added, turning to his friend, who was sharing a prison cell with him.

'Faith, I cannot tell. All I know is that I will never forsake you.'

'Yet Cunégonde has forsaken me. Alas, a wife has not the worth of a friend, what though he be a mestizo.'

Soon after this Candide and Cacambo were taken back to Copenhagen, where Candide expected a dreadful fate. He was, as it proved, mistaken. What awaited him at Copenhagen was not doom, but happiness. Immediately on his arrival he learnt that Volhall was dead. Nobody mourned for this cruel and brutal man.

In Candide, on the contrary, everyone was keenly interested. He was unfettered and set at liberty, and was able at once to hasten to his Zenoida. At first they could hardly speak for emotion, but only wept and kissed. Cacambo, who was present at their meeting, was almost as much affected as his friend.

'Dear Cacambo, adorable Zenoida!' said Candide, 'you efface from my heart the deep traces of my misfortunes. Love and friendship hold in store for me days of serenity and moments of delight. To reach this unexpected bliss, through how many trials have I passed! But they are all forgot. Dear Zenoida, I behold you once more, and you love me. Everything is for the best, everything in Nature is good.'

Volhall's death left Zenoida mistress of her own fortunes. The Court gave her a pension from her father's confiscated estate, and this she shared with Candide and Cacambo. She lodged them in her house, telling everyone that she was under a deep debt of gratitude to these two foreigners, and for this reason wished to provide them with the comforts and pleasures of life, so as to make up to them for all the misfortunes they had suffered.

Some people saw through this statement; which was not very difficult, seeing that Zenoida's previous connection with Candide had been a public scandal. The majority blamed her, but a few thinking people approved of her conduct.

Zenoida, who was not entirely indifferent to the opinion of fools, was somewhat unhappy. Cunégonde's death, however—news of which reached Copenhagen through the Jesuit trading factory—enabled Zenoida to rehabilitate herself in popular favour. She had a genealogy drawn up for Candide, which ingeniously traced his descent from one of the oldest families in Europe. The genealogist even claimed that Candide's real name was Canute, which was the name of one of the Kings of Denmark. This was found entirely credible, as *dide* into *ute* is not a great metamorphosis. By means of this little change Candide became a great lord. He married Zenoida publicly, and they lived as happily as anyone can expect to live. Cacambo became Zenoida's friend as well as Candide's. Candide would often say: 'Everything is not so good as in El Dorado; but everything is not too bad.'

WORDSWORTH CLASSICS

General Editors: Marcus Clapham and Clive Reynard
Other titles in this series

Pride and Prejudice
Wuthering Heights
Alice in Wonderland
Father Brown - Selected Stories
Great Expectations
Tess of the d'Urbervilles
Women in Love
Moby Dick
Hamlet
Twelfth Night
Tom Sawyer & Huckleberry Finn
Oliver Twist
The Last of the Mohicans
Romeo and Juliet
The Picture of Dorian Gray
Sense and Sensibility
The Wind in the Willows
Othello
Vanity Fair
Jane Eyre
Tom Jones
Julius Caesar
Frankenstein
David Copperfield
The Odyssey
Call of the Wild & White Fang
Gulliver's Travels
Emma
Dracula
The Scarlet Letter
Persuasion
The Return of
Sherlock Holmes
A Midsummer Night's Dream
20,000 Leagues under the Sea
Mansfield Park

The Adventures of
Sherlock Holmes
The Ambassadors
Macbeth
Don Quixote
Lord Jim
The Red Badge of Courage
A Tale of Two Cities
The Three Musketeers
The Great Gatsby
Richard II
Treasure Island
The Moonstone
Robinson Crusoe
Cranford
Sons and Lovers
Canterbury Tales
Tales of Mystery and Imagination
Les Miserables
Three Men in a Boat
Pickwick Papers
Ghost Stories
Plain Tales From the Hills
Richard III
The Riddle of the Sands
Northanger Abbey
Fanny Hill
The Dubliners
As You Like It
Lord Arthur Savile's Crime
The Merchant of Venice
War and Peace
Shirley
The Secret Agent
Far from the Madding Crowd
Dr. Jekyll and Mr. Hyde

Distribution

AUSTRALIA, BRUNEI
& MALAYSIA
Treasure Press
22 Salmon Street
Port Melbourne, Vic 3207
Tel: (03) 646 6716
Fax: (03) 646 6925

DENMARK
BOG-FAN
St. Kongensgade 61A
1264 København K

BOGPA SIKA
Industrivej 1
7120 Vejle Ø

FRANCE
Bookking International
16 Rue Des Grands Augustins
75006 Paris, France

GERMANY, AUSTRIA
& SWITZERLAND
Swan Buch-Marketing GmbH
Goldscheuerstrabe 16
D-7640 Kehl Am Rhein
Germany

GREAT BRITAIN & IRELAND
Wordsworth Editions Ltd
8B East Street, Ware
Herts SG12 9HU

Selecta Books
The Selectabook Distribution Centre
Folly Road, Roundway, Devizes
Wilts SN10 2HR

HOLLAND & BELGIUM
Uitgeverlj En Boekhandel
Van Gennep BV
Spuistraat 283
1012 VR Amsterdam, Holland

ITALY
Magis Books
Piazza Della Vittoria 1/C
42100 Reggio Emilia
Tel: 0522-452303
Fax: 0522-452845

NEW ZEALAND
Whitcoulls Limited
Private Bag 92098
Auckland, New Zealand

NORWAY
Norsk Bokimport AS
Bertrand Narvesensvei 2
Postboks 6219, Etterstad
0602 Oslo, Norway

SINGAPORE
Book Station
18 Leo Drive
Singapore
Tel: 4511998
Fax: 4529188

SOUTH AFRICA
Trade Winds Press (Pty) Ltd
P O Box 20194
Durban North 4016
South Africa

SWEDEN
Akademibokhandelsgruppen
Box 21002
100 31 Stockholm